mostly womenfolk and a man or two:

a collection

MIGNON HOLLAND ANDERSON

Third World Press

They are sweet and angry
and strong here. . .
They are fallen here, buried here,
Mostly men.
And we who survive are
Mostly womenfolk and a man or two. . . .

dedication

To Mom, Ruby Holland Lynk, and
to Mon Père, William A. Lynk,
for all of the love and the
support and the faith which
made me grow up loving life
and people and dreaming dreams
of my own. . . .

A very special thank you

To John Oliver Killens,
for telling me as many times
as I needed to hear it,
to listen to my own heart
and to write. . . .
And to Grace Killens,
for her continuing interest
and support and friendship. . . .

The Setting Of All Events Herein

Way back, in times promised and in times gone forever and spent into vagueness, the "Eastern Shore" has sat like a shaft of unharvested wheat between ocean and bay, marking the beginning and the end of the Chesapeake.

Her memorable history began with the settling of native peoples from the north and from across the continent's western shore, people called Accomac, who named her creeks and necks of land Occahonnock, Puncateague, Matta and Onancock. They fished from her banks and raised a culture which flourished for generations without interruption.

John Smith set foot on her and brought with him a seemingly shy age of paleness from a world he and others like him would presume to be more ancient, civilized and glorious. In a relatively short time her narrowest fifty miles would be renamed Virginia according to a faraway royal edict, and all that she had been would be transformed, her original inhabitants all but forgotten beneath the march of colonization, wars, slavery and the haunting trials of emancipation.

CONTENTS

Born A Child To Struggle And To Die

Birth and death live near one another like neighbors in the city, back to back, and in between the thin space where their bones rub at time, are all of the emotions, all of the actions, events, stages which are the human experience. The infant was once in utero, the child was once a tiny cry in its mother's arms. Men and women, young and fertile, were all once children. The old, once young, stare forward at death and back at a past gone forever despite dreams and projections. Whether in repose or fighting with flailing arms and bitter words, it is from the beginning to the end the same chain linked to itself—this living and dying that we do.

And yet no day is the same and if we are fortunate and blessed we have hope for better days. *There is* a difference between the first days and the last, between living and dying, between men and women. It is not a difference in right to aspire, however. For all of us who lived the misery of being made to be something other than what we were; for all of us now living who picked cotton and bore children unwanted and still find ourselves in strange fields and lying on cold beds, there are changes still due and coming. If we make the differences count for something, and only if.

born

when the baby got going

So many times we laid there in the dark and held each other, parting when sleep made us turn. I often bathed him after, a warm soapy cloth, a warm wet fresh water cloth, a dry soft towel. By then his eyes would be heavy with sleep. He would grin at me sometimes, still shy at being bathed by a woman, yet delighted and spoiled.

One night, (I like to think it was on this particular night that our son began) in his eyes, clear to me in the soft light shed by the lantern, I saw tears, not at all sad, well up. He laughed, shaking his head, jumped up with me somehow in his arms, and I'm not a small woman, and held me cradled there. He walked, carrying me and said, "Whatever else there is in this crazy world, given the walls, and the downs and the ups and the inbetweens, you make me free. Ah, momma, you make me free." My body, I think on that night, began to change for a nine month spell and we ceased to be just two.

momma's child

Once upon a time, Poppa entered deeply into Momma, many many nights ago, and left his part of me. I am here now, inside of Momma where it is warm and downright hot sometimes. She carries me low, deep inside the girdle beneath her belly.

Last night she turned over in bed after she had been quiet for a long time. I rocked with her movement. She frowned. The paint on the ceiling was peeling in large erratic strips. Her sister, a little thing years ago, had eaten such paint in another house and had died. I could feel her thoughts—Would the leaded paint one day poison me when she wasn't watching as its ugliness now poisoned the look of her house? Momma looked away.

My father was there. I had known for almost an hour that he was still awake and restless and struggling to find sleep. His stomach growled emptily.

A sensation slipped over her, over me, as she rolled into his arms and then a warm comfort enveloped us.

"Can't sleep?" Her eyes took in full view of his face in the half light. He had been young once; only a year or two before.

"Naw." He caressed her face, letting his hand fall back limply upon his side. She was so near her time and he didn't have money enough for a doctor. The doctor knew it and said unless he saw money in hand he wouldn't come.

Jim broke out in a sweat whenever he allowed himself to remember the things he knew about midwives; how so few he had heard of knew anything beyond the barest essentials about childbirth. Infection. Women dead and gone.

Momma eased closer and kissed him, holding him all the while with a tender kneading of her fingers, stroking, bringing him toward full stir. His stomach rumbled.

"Ah, Lord," he said.

"You needs to eat more," she pleaded. "I hear your stomach growling and cramping."

Poppa chuckled, amused at the fact that Momma's closeness, her hands, had shifted his mind way below his stomach's need now, hot all over as he was, throbbing.

"I'm talking about your stomach," she said. "You do need to eat more." They laughed, but the concern in her voice deepened. "I kin work."

"No."

"Not the first time a pregnant woman was working right up to her time. Shucks, black slave women even fought slavery with guns and axes between carrying and labor pains. Great grandma Ames done that and her baby, Granpa Tobby, was in the world three whole days when they hung her."

"No." He drew the word out softly. "You had one time to faint. Don't want that baby born dead or you ruined like some old mare worked to a plow too long. Naw. You'se worked right hard already." He stroked the back of her head, slipping his hand softly over her hair, down to the base of her neck and down. As he touched her, he sighed, growing full. She was so warm these days with carrying the child. Woke up sometimes wringing wet. And under the film of water her flesh was firm, the muscles lightly defined when she flexed them so that he felt as much or more heat rising in himself as when her belly was flat and childless.

He didn't have many words to give to her. Life frightened them both in the same way. They both could remember the same shadows over things; the hunger which hovered in their heads when they were young: three and four years old, and which only seemed to come from their stomachs alone; the way the air tasted, musty and repugnant, whenever the white man came for the rent money, and the way things seemed to remain because he always seemed to be there, hovering like hunger. Jim remembered the jar of honey which sat on his aunt's work table in the kitchen where she cooked and cooked and cooked all day for the strange smelling white man. The jar was as big as Jim's head, big around, and a bee comb floated in it. He watched the jar being tilted, honey flowing over breads and cakes and into mixes of good things, covering dishes and spoons. He watched, wondering how it was that the jar never emptied; wondering how the golden liquid slow to move, must taste, and tasting one day off of a discarded spoon which Aunt Sarah forgot to put out of reach. He watched for longer hours after that, stomach cramps bubbling stronger for want of the sweet honey he was forbidden to eat, until one day somewhere during the age of five he reached above his head, alone in the kitchen, and precariously pulled the heavy glass barrier to his joy toward the edge of the table. It came reluctantly at a creep, heavy and promising, and gave him such a laboring hard time that when it was finally in his arms and sitting between his legs on the floor he had no need to muster greater effort to screw the tin lid off. It came away and he dipped his spoon and ate and ate and lost all sense of where he was or how long the shadows were until his Aunt's fell upon him, the spoon in mid-dip and the jar one third empty. When he saw her, he slowly raised the sticky spoon, squinted his eyes and cried in screams of fright which even now he could feel and taste for all the years gone by.

A grieving sound escaped his open mouth, so my Momma went right on holding him, kneading, and worked her loving black woman's art, holding him almost like a child from where she lay on her heavy side, breathing all of her life into him, working the grief away and trying to say with her body that she understood and becoming a woman, strong, proud, eager, shy somehow and mellow and young like the first time it was really good. Like the first times when he gave her lessons on long nights beneath the quilt her grandma Haynes had made piece by piece. Poppa moved into her and his manliness overcame her.

"Lord, Jim, I swear to God," she shouted and he stroked slow, coming out almost, teasing and then down deep toward me, stripping fire, telling me how this manchild should one day be a loving man, holding a woman soft with child and respectful like and hard.

There was such a tenderness in his way, in his slow sensuous feeling of her, around and up, away and in again. Hard, sweaty, funky friction, slow to going mad.

Momma screamed and took to trembling all over and Daddy came, breathing up a storm, to rest inside of her, the curve of her belly carving an arc across the hard front of his belly. I grew calm and slept as they slept, for the first time in many hours.

the sizing tree

Part I

The girl arrived in the middle of the first night of November, 1910, about as noisy a child as the Evers family had welcomed in its history. "Didn't even have to slap her behind to get her going," was what her father bragged to friends and family all the next day. "That girl is her great grandmother all over again."

"Yes, indeed," his wife, Sara, said, smiling in her bed, weak from labor but deeply satisfied. "Jacob, we'll call her Nora. Nora Lyman Evers after her great grandma."

Uncle Thurston, Jacob's twin, was the self proclaimed poet in the family. He was a tall, bordering on skinny, man with deeply set eyes, bushy eyebrows, a full mouth, a heavy shock of straight to curly black hair which fell lazy across his head, blue eyes and a soft dark brown complexion. People were always a little surprised when they looked into his dark narrow face and saw those blazing blue eyes. Some whites said it was unnatural, but then too, they didn't know the Evers' family history.

Sara was his favorite sister-in-law of the wives among his four brothers. He fidgited beside the potbellied stove in the settin' room for half of the night, listening to Sara moan with labor, and when he heard the baby cry out, he stood up like a shot and yelled, "Great God, it's a baby sho' 'nuf," startling everyone else in the room to their feet. He continued to shout excitedly. "I said tonight was the night, just after the stroke of twelve, and look yonder at the clock-12:03 a.m.—indeed I was right."

"God damn, Thurston," his brother Albert yelled. "You crazy. Sit down man, for God's sake, scare me to death." Everybody, his sisters Annie and Wilhelmena, brothers Thomas, William and Albert, all laughed, relieved by all of the screaming that little Nora was doing and congratulating each other as eagerly as if they were the parents themselves.

Jacob shook his head, laughing, as he leaned back into the room from looking at his baby. "I feel that way too, Thurston. You've got to write something down about this here night. Your baby sister-in-law has born her first daughter and she's a picture to behold. And Lord have mercy, I'm the daddy. I swear, I feel like I ain't never done nothing like this before."

"Well," Thurston chimed in, "seeing as how this is the first baby girl Sara has birthed, this sho' better be the first time you've done something like this before or you better keep it a secret." The room exploded with laughter and Jacob turned a little red in the face. "Go on now, Thurs," Wilhelmena said. "Jest because you'se got all them children scattered over tarnation...."

"None a that, Willie. Let me see that child before I get in deep here." Thurston chuckled, patted Jacob on the back, ran his fingers through his hair so he would look halfway neat and plunged through the curtain which draped the bedroom doorway. As he neared Sara he became a little shy and simply stood over her for a moment. Sara beamed up at him. "You look fit to bust," Thurston said. She was a lovely sight lying there with the baby wrapped snugly in her arms. "No, **brother, I look terrible. I know I must." Thurston** studied her face for a second. "You look tired, yes, but you're beautiful just the same." He kissed Sara on the tip of her nose, something he had done many times, and peeked at Nora beneath her covers. "So this is what all that loving lead to, huh. Well little sister, you done good."

"She's born perfect, Thurs." Sara's voice was weak, like she was congested. She coughed and closed her eyes in pain. Thurston looked toward the midwife and back, rather fearful that something was wrong.

"You hurting?"

"It's never easy, but I'm fine. You give me a few days of Mrs. Wilks' care and I'll be my old self." She smiled reassuringly. "Go get Jacob off his feet so he can rest. He's been up mostly two days now."

"OK. I'm going. Mrs. Wilks, you look after her now." He moved toward the door, just worried enough not to smile. He loved Sara dearly and had wished many a time that he had met her before Jacob. He had never **shared these feelings with anyone and would have been** ashamed to admit it, but at a time like this, his longing for her made him feel that he had missed out on the most precious part of his life.

Sara watched him go, so much like Jacob in the shape of his silhouetted head and back, and she wondered beneath exhaustion how it would be with Nora. How Nora would be without a mother to rear her.

Jacob's eyes were tightly shut, but he could see every object in the room, and he wondered why it was that

Sara was gone. The night outside was thick and cold with winter. All of the stars he could see in a lifetime were spread across the sky, like they had been since they came into the world. The same trees. The same pond. The same stones. The foundation logs of the house the same. It was all there except for her.

His chair creaked to the rhythm of his weight as he studied his life.

"Jacob, Jacob, you got to make arrangements," a voice kept saying in his head. "She's been dead going on two days, now. You got to put her to rest and let air into the house. Miss Lottie kain't keep on with your children like she's been if you don't get Sara out of that bed and into the ground."

He was a young man. The hair on his head was black and heavy with ringlets like curled silk falling into his eyes from not being brushed in place the way she liked to see it. He had assumed that she would always be with him. He wondered when he first learned that she was dying if he could love the baby. "If I give you a girl, Jacob, then we won't have any more children." He knew somewhere into this seventh day of Nora's life that loving her would be close to the most impossible thing he could conceive of and do. His mind was swollen with a pain which would not let him move to even comfort the tiny thing when she cried.

The house was way old and bent in places where the slave cabin log foundation had given in to time. Three rooms downstairs, three rooms on the second floor. They had always seemed enough. But now it seemed to him that they were a pitiful offering to a woman who had died giving him a child. The oil lantern was burning black smoke. Its heavy yellow light barely touched his face. He remembered and remembered.

"Sara, I spoke with Doctor Ashley yestidy in Eastville. He said I was to call him when your time was close.

Said he'd take a sow for his trouble."

She stood by the wood stove pouring griddle batter into a large ironware skillet. Sara was rather tall, five foot six, and thin except for her middle where the baby was. She wiped sweat from her face and flipped the cakes over with a spatula, all the while shaking her head.

"No Jake, I think we'll have Miz Wilks over to do the birthing, like the three children before. I trust her and I know her and I don't want Doctor Ashley."

"Sara, it's the best thing. Mrs. Wilks don't know much if anything goes wrong. I've been scared everytime that something would go wrong."

"Now Jacob, my mind is set." She paused and pulled the skillet to the side of the stove onto the warming oven lid. "I don't mean to worry you." She sighed. "How many hotcakes you think you can eat?"

"Why you got to be so stubborn, Sara?" His voice seemed to have moved across something detestable. She could have sworn that the sentence smashed into the walls. He stood up and lost his temper. "Dr. Ashley's gonna birth this last child and that's that. Do you hear?"

"I don't hear no such thing." Sara turned with her hands on her hips, her back to him and her attention somewhere off, waiting for him to relent.

He turned to go, angry and confused that Sara could be so obstinate. "Sara, I'm thinking it would be best if you had a doctor this time. I'm thinking you should."

"Jacob, it's me that'll pass this baby into the world and I want Mrs. Wilks. Now go on and wash up for breakfast."

And so he did.

Part II

When Jacob left the kitchen, Sara felt the need to sit down, not because she was tired or suffering from her five months of pregnancy; not because she was upset or angry in any way, but because she could not quite understand herself. Her tone with Jacob had been much more stern than she had intended. Why was it that she didn't want Dr. Ashley? She knew herself to be a modern, thinking woman. She had been attended by doctors before and nurses, most of them white. The first time she ever stepped into a doctor's office was at the Hampton Institution where she was a student. Sara smiled. She had met Jacob on a Wednesday in the dining hall after the original seating arrangements had been changed for supper. He was studying the blacksmith trade and worked like the devil to catch her eye everytime he passed the food. They were engaged by the following Tuesday. It was a lovely time, being young and at Hampton and courting.

The baby moved. Sara unconsciously patted her abdomen and thought again about the present. Was it because Dr. Ashley was white? Yes, that was part of it, but it was deeper. It had something to do with his strangeness and the strangeness of his kind. He reminded her of all of those familiar things which brought fear and the sting of the unfamiliar. And what was strange was empty of meaning, void like the darkness when you didn't know where you were and you had no memory of how things looked in the light because you had never seen them and had always been afraid of emptiness. She didn't know Dr. Ashley's hands, nor the shape of his personality. Nothing about him had ever touched her except perhaps that part which was unknown and shrouded in darkness. She couldn't see him in her imagination. He was the harshness in her past which had no name: the cultural inheritance she would sooner forget than touch. Mrs. Wilks was home and comfort.

The cold of winter when she stood and met it head on was exhilerating to her, even in memory. But the creeping chill of a damp fireless winter house brought on aches deep in her joints, in the places where she bent to move. Here was a coldness which had taken over her body many times. Yet it was strange to her. She couldn't quite identify it, especially indoors, in her bed or down the hallways, where it lurked at full strength. Dr. Ashley was a cold winter house where the fire had long since gone out.

Over an hour passed while she sat there thinking, puzzling over the strangeness. She came back to the kitchen with as great a sense of shock as if she had been transported there without her knowledge from another room. There were chores to do and Lottie Philips, the neighbor lady who helped her with the children and other things about the house, would soon be back from the store. Lottie reminded Sara of a girl she had roomed with in school; a girl named Carol Blake. Lottie and Carol were both of the same build and dark complexion and both had a poor look about them; a neglected look which showed subtlely in their faces and carriage. She and Carol had been great friends during the first few months at Hampton, taking classes together and sewing together in the evenings, until the day came in January when Jacob started coming to call. Carol became very cold and hostile and after awhile she began making remarks. "I tell you, if my hair was straight like yours, Sara, you wouldn't have a chance with Jacob. He'd be mine. His head's just turned by your high yella and long grass." Sara finally decided to room with someone else.

Lottie said almost nothing out loud, but Sara could tell by the way she looked at Jacob that she wanted him for herself. Lottie often worked in the fields with Jacob. *Lottie surely did* and knowing the Evers men, it worried Sara. Jacob, God fearing or not, might be tempted on a warm day to follow Lottie's lead.

This baby would be a girl. Sara thought about it often enough to make it so. Of course, sometimes she wondered if it would be fair to have a girl. The poor little thing would find the world a mighty hard place.

Men had the best places and were as ignorant as mule skinners about women. There were so many little considerations that they never got around to thinking. As good a man as Jacob was, he often forgot the meaning of the children to her life. Her ambitions were soaring when she finished her course at Hampton. There she was, a fine seamstress with great ideas in her head about opening a store in Eastville with handmade dresses and frills. Jacob didn't think it was a good idea; said something about needing help on the farm and not wanting her working in public like that where white men might take it upon themselves to keep her company and there would be babies, he wanted children right away. She had still hoped, but once she was pregnant it became impossible. Even now, somedays, when she was working on a lovely dress for some white woman, or for one of the women among the three prosperous coloured families in the county, she saw herself in a clean pretty shop, meeting gay people who would marvel at her skill and make her days full of the kind of excitement that she remembered from school. Some days she found it hard to be cheerful. It was as if some part of her, somewhere near her soul, had been stunted and made awful to live with. Jacob was right and she was wrong. She would be vulnerable; but what of her dreams and her talent? It was ignorance. Nothing but small mindedness and ignorance that made a victim of her because she was a black woman.

Mrs. Wilkes was ignorant too of many things. She was a good enough soul full of outlandish stories and gossip and kind in her way. Her training as a midwife was as good as self-training and work among simple country folk could be, Sara supposed, but there were many things which trial and error could not teach in time. Jacob's fear that "something could go wrong" as he had put it, might be well founded. It might be, but her fear of that possibility was not as severe as her fear of Dr. Ashley's hands.

Part III

Jake Evers had his forty acres, not fully paid for, and one mule, one horse, a boar, two sows, four shoats and a small flock of chickens that he did own, feathers and tail. All and all given the fact that farmers weren't getting much for their labor, he was a poor man who seemed, because there was so little for so many, to be well off. Times were hard for most folk on the Eastern Shore of Virginia, and mostly impossible for the coloured population. Hunting rabbit, quail, coon and such kept body and soul from going their separate ways during the winter months, but even so, life was a naturally hard struggle everyday. There had been too much rain during the spring of 1910 and too much dry summer heat when the land needed showers. Plants drowned and rotted at their roots or scorched from their tops straight down to the ground. It seemed to him that his children looked more than ever like scarecrows and there was too much work for him everyday to give Sara anything except more hard work.

When all of the folk cleared out at the end of that first day of his baby daughter's life, the house grew quiet and restful. It seemed like a palace. Sara and baby Nora were tucked warmly under their covers. The midwife was snoozing on a cot at the foot of the big bed, in case Sara should need her. His three sons were quiet in bed and dreaming. The feasting was over, the house was clean and the first cold of winter was shut out at the door. All Jake could hear, sitting in his wife's rocking chair, was the light creak of its wood to the rhythm of his peaceful soul and the blowing of the wind against the chimney flue. He felt satisfied. He felt like a part of creation. It was over, Sara was fine and he could go on.

He remembered the last twenty-four hours, the earliest of them when he was worried sick that Sara would have complications. He knew Mrs. Wilks could feel his distrust. Recognition of his feelings showed in his eyes. Several times he almost left the house and struck out for Dr. Ashley. But he knew it would take hours to travel the twenty miles in a buggy, and if he was going to have the doctor there, he should have sent for him the day before. Everybody said it would be all right. Mrs. Wilks was good at her trade and Sara was strong. He waivered in making the decision and finally decided to go with Sara's judgment. The old lady had delivered the first three. Why not this one.

He sat in the quiet and remembered things he hadn't touched in his mind since they happened or he had heard about them. Jacob didn't usually drink, but on this night he felt the need for a nip. He knew better than to take more than one good jigger. Two drinks brought on wild dreams, and more than that brought on nightmares. He knew better than to drink, just as he knew better than to trust Mrs. Wilks, but he was doing both despite what he knew. Maybe the one was because of the other. Yes. He knew that was so. Tonight the drinking wouldn't matter. It could only help him get over the darkness. Maybe by morning the baby would be born and he could relax. It was a wonder that all of his relatives weren't sitting around the house with him. The house had been full during the last two nights before his third son was born. Maybe tomorrow. Jacob sipped and thought and dreamed and grew uneasy in his chair. And then he passed into sleep and summertime, 1898, and the day when he first heard the legend, and for awhile he slept calmly.

From the time Jacob's Uncle Elija took him out there, he thought about her. He learned to masterbate thinking about her. She made his blood hot, even now that he was twenty-five years old and seven years older than when she stopped coming to him and now about to see his fourth child born. He first heard of her a few months after he came into puberty. He was thirteen and his body had begun to feel strange. He noticed the new hair growing under his arms and down around his crotch and he felt a soreness for several weeks around his tits. At first he was scared to death that his chest was going to sprout breasts like his sister's, but they never did, and then the soreness went away and he forgot to worry about it. His mind and his body turned more to girls, to women and their secrets. Things that his mother said and things that the preacher said made him feel ashamed about what he thought whenever he thought of girls, but he kept on thinking anyway, wondering if there wasn't something awful in him. He thought about the story Uncle Elija told him and he made many trips through the back lot woods to look at it again. Many a time he wanted to climb the trunk to see what would happen, but the more he hesitated, the more he feared finding out. His dreams were perfection and he didn't dare tarnish them with the possibility of an empty reality.

On that first day, he and Elija stood beneath the massive oak and stared. It looked ordinary to him, except for its unusually great size and the way the main trunk divided into three huge branches about thirty feet above the ground. The branches curved out smoothly away from the center of the trunk and then struck straight upwards, forming a triangle at their base. When they were heavy with leaves they made a secluded and restful covering above the space which lay between them.

"It's up there that it happens," his uncle said. "Up

there where the main trunk branches off in three directions forming a couch in the middle. There's room up there for a man to stretch out right comfortable." Jacob strained to see. He had heard some of the stories and expected a whole lot more than nature was providing at the moment. "The strange thing is right there," Elija said, trying not to let Jacob see him grinning, and pointing straight up the face of the main trunk at a place where it rounded between two of the branches. "You see there, boy. There's a small hole right there as you climb up between. They say you have to climb naked; that the charm of the Sizing Tree won't come to you if any part of you body is covered, and you have to be a Black man." Jacob pulled his bottom lip unconsciously, thinking about being naked up that tree.

"Je-sus," he said, knowing it was all right to speak of the Lord casually when he was with Elija. Elija was his mother's favorite brother and what he did was always mostly right. "Won't you skin yourself or git ant bit or something?"

Elija strained not to laugh. "Not in that tree, boy. Not if you climb when the sun is high. The woman will protect you."

"What woman? Unc, you pulling my leg?"

"Naw, Jake, I'm not lying to you." Elija smiled up at the tree. "I've never had the spunk to climb up there myself. I thought about it many a time, but I always got cold feet. Then too, I figured somebody might come along and catch me with my tail hanging out."

Jacob chuckled with delight. "What's that hole for and what woman you talking about?

"It's for a man's balls." Elija laughed, guffawed a note or two in fact and shook his head at his lack of control. "The story goes that if you'se a boy, your balls will fall into the hole when you stretch out up there head to tail, but if you'se a full man, they'll be too big to drop in. If you'se half way between and never been loved by a woman, you'll get your balls caught and only the woman can set you free. You've got to be ripe for loving so to speak, and more trusting than a holyman."

"Je-sus, is that true?"

"'Course its true." And then Elija turned Jacob around and started him walking back through the woods toward the house. "Now you see, another thing that always worried me was this. What if there was a squirrel or a wood pecker in that hole. A man's nuts kain't take but so much, you know. Getting your oysters shucked ain't my idea of loving." A few steps away from the tree and Elija was finding it hard to stay on his feet, he was laughing so hard. Jacob had to rest against a pine tree to wait for Elija to get himself together.

"Come on Uncle Elija. You jest brought me out here to make a joke. Tell me the story anyhow."

"Oouueee, Jacob," Elija said wiping his eyes. "It's one hell of a story. I guess it's time you heard it." It took awhile, but by the time they reached the house, Jacob was downright fascinated and a lot more knowledgeable. His Uncle told him the story in great detail.

The slave ship entered Cape Charles harbor in the early spring of 1842. The town was bustling with trade and the white people were eager to get a look at the cargo. Sixteen slaves were landed and immediately readied for sale, all of them young, three of them female and all of them pure African. They were straight from Africa, except for a brief stop in the west Indies. They spoke the barest of English and huddled together, afraid, during the auction.

"What am I bid for this fine buck, Kwame, seventeen year old and sturdy. Lookathim folks, lookathim. Good bone and muscle from head to toe. Good for working, good for breeding. Take off them clothes boy and let these fine ladies and gentlemen see you whole."

White men and women, fashionably dressed, poor and in between stood close upon the block, shouting at the boy to remove his pants. Hands reached out to force him. Men wrestled him down, ripped his pants off and balanced him back onto his feet. A rustle of appreciation went through the crowd; the boy was magnificent. He stared, every nerve tight with rage and helplessness.

"What amIbid, what amIbid for this prettylittle thing, Efua, daughter of an African King, fine brown thing what-amI bid. Don't be ashamed girl, take off them rags so's all these gents can lay eyes on you. Don't do no good to cry. Get out a whip if you don't do what you're told."

And just like that the two of them and fourteen others were sold. They were promised to each other, but had seen little of each other during the crossing. It was a miracle that both were alive. Some seven hundred souls had begun the trip from their homeland. They were packed into slots side by side and one upon the other. Fresh air was nonexistant and illness overcame just about everybody. Some weren't strong enough to begin with. A few broke away and threw themselves into the sea. Nineteen were killed by crewmen during a rebellion. Many strong ones died.

One young girl, fifteen years old, gave birth to a premature infant in the hold. Kwame could still hear her screams. None of the women could crawl into a position to help her. Shortly after the baby was born, crewmen examined the helpless pair and took them away. The mother was too weak, they said, to make the remainder of the journey, and the child would require too much care. Not one of the crew seemed to mind as they told of how the captain ordered them overboard. "You get sick and you're shark bait. A sick slave is a dead nigger," was all. Four hundred and eighty-one lived to reach the new world for sale.

Kwame watched the white woman who had bought Efua taking her away and he shouted his vow to her in their native language. They would be together again before the waning of the next full moon, or die.

Efua was taken to live in Onancock while Kwame lived in a house on the outskirts of Cape Charles. On the night of the first new moon, they both stole away from their masters and started the thirty mile trip toward each other. Kwame traveling due north, Efua first east and then due south. After three days they met, as if by some miracle, at the foot of what was to become The Sizing Tree. "It's over," he said, "We're free now."

"They'll come," she said. "They'll surely come and kill us."

"No they won't, Efua. There's magic in this place and in us. We cannot be harmed in this land anymore. We are the spirits of love among our people."

Their clothes were torn and dirty and they were exhausted, but otherwise fine. They could not understand how they had found each other in such a thick forest, but were too enchanted with each other to do other than thank their ancestors for seeing them safely back together.

The tree seemed to beckon to them. There was even a ladder made of vines for their use. "No we must bathe first," he said, leading her by the hand. "This is our wedding night, Efua. The waters must cleanse us." And surely enough, not far distant, they found a fresh spring and each one standing watch for the other, they bathed and refreshed themselves. When they returned to the tree they found a natural bed between the branches. Kwame stretched out across the rough bark and eased Efua's body down over him. Giving warmth to each other, they fell into a deep sleep.

It was well into the morning of the next day when they awoke. Kwame opened his eyes to the peaceful morning quiet of the forest and found Efua balanced easily on one of the branches by his leg. She smiled down at him and gave him fresh grapes which she had gathered from wild vines near the forest floor. That she had climbed down the great trunk and ascended again alone just to feed him was marvelous. He lay on his back, smiling and eating and enchanted, not at all thoughtful of where he was.

It was then that he noticed that he was caught in the tree. His pants were torn and his testicles had fallen into the hole. He was small enough to fall in, but too large to come out again without injuring himself. For a moment he paniced.

"Lie back," she said, "I'll free you. Lie still." Resting by his head against one of the branches was a small jug which neither of them had seen before. The wind breathed for a second through the leaves of the tree, and then, as though she had received secret instructions, Efua took the jug, removed the clay and cork stopper and poured a red liquid into her hand. It was an oil, light to the touch and fragrant with the odor of strawberries.

The sun filtered down to them through the leaves and a warm breeze caressed their faces. A cloud passed over the sun, darkening the forest black. When the light returned, they were both naked and magnificent to each other's eyes.

"I will free you," said Efua. "Whenever you are imprisoned,I will set you free." Beginning at his eyes, her hands moved across his face, leaving the light scent of strawberries over his skin. Her mouth followed her hands, the hands caressing, kneading, her mouth sucking away the delicious oil as she moved down across his body, stirring him to sensations he had never known. She set him on fire from his head to his toes, licking, biting, sucking her way down. The oil rolled into his navel and her tongue came and swept it away. His stomach sucked in and his penis stood up, tapping her in the throat. "So soft," she whispered. "So hard and soft." The oil flowed abundantly down and she licked further, following it past the strong growth of hair until she came to the root of his penis, slid her mouth upwards and took it in all of its fullness into her mouth.

Kwame shuddered and sighed with pleasure, reached down and caressed her face and then sucked in his belly again. She filled her mouth with him, sucking him into her, then blowing him out again, never letting go, up and down squeezing the head with her lips, slipping over wet and slippery, plunging down around upon him again and again, faster and faster, up and down, twisting him, drawing him at a furious pace until he screamed with the surging of his seed in great jerks like he would explode again and again forevermore. And all the while the strawberry oil flowed around him like wine and she ate it away, lubricating him lower and lower until his testicles were, with the help of her hands, free from harm. They rested and then Kwame made love to Efua with all of the power in his young body, consumating their marriage in the full circle of giving which she had begun.

She lay asleep in his arms for hours, more beautiful than he had imagined. He had seen her naked from the waist up many times in their village where it was the custom among his people for women to walk uncovered. A wrap of handwoven cloth had been worn about her hips. It had touched her legs lightly and showed the shape of her coming womanhood whenever she moved. Now he knew how truly lovely she was. Kwame opened his eyes and forced himself to think beyond the spell of their loving. It was time he found them food. The weight of his responsibility fell with a sudden heaviness over his spirits.

"Efua," he said. "Wake up, Efua." He helped her to her feet, and as he turned to find their clothers, they heard voices and looking down, saw the muzzle of a gun pointing at them. Kwame's hand closed tightly around Efua's hand and in that instant the two lovers disappeared, dissolving before the eyes of the men who had come to take away their freedom. They vanished, some said, into the wood of the tree, the strawberry oil jug with them. Wherever they went, they were never seen again by white men, and the black men who stood helplessly among the white slavers, told of the couple and dreamed of her. Some said they later loved and were loved by her.

It came to be said that the right man, young and black but not too young, nor old, but just so, could become Kwame as he was on his wedding day, and if he climbed the Tree, would be caught and freed again by Efua. It was said that the right black woman, budding with youthful beauty and a love full of faith and imagination, if she climbed the Tree, would become Efua, freeing her Kwame and winning his love and companionship forever.

On and on in his dreams, the fantasies of early dawn just before waking, Jacob as Kwame, Kwame as Jacob. Mornings and weeks and parts of years passing, him stretched naked above the ground with Efua in his arms. Those first dreams were failures. He was too small. Too young. Finally, there came a day when he too, like Kwame became Kwame and was trapped. The aroma of strawberries whipped pungent on the wind and Efua came. They loved each other in

his daydreams over and over, time upon time, for
three summers, well into his eighteenth year.
Unexpectedly the day came when Efua came no more.

Something unforgivable happened between them early
on the last morning they spent together. He was
Kwame and yet very much himself. In his mind his
body was deep black as Kwame's had been, his hair
was kinky and thick. The fact that his body was really
pale and only brown where his shirt stayed open
and his arms were exposed during the summer never
contradicted the black form in his dreams. The fact
that his hair was really straight never came to light,
until that last morning when he stretched out waiting
for her and he looked down and saw that his body
looked like a white man's. He struggled in his sleep
against the vision and remembered, despite his efforts
to close his mind, all the things he had heard about
light skinned Negroes and all the good and terrible
things he had experienced as a light skinned coloured
man. He had been proud of looking white, and yet he
had been ambivolent. Being black in color was
frowned upon by most of his family, by white people
and even by some black people. His twin brother,
Thurston, was just like him except for complexion.
Their faces looked the same except Thurston was dark
brown and he was white and all of their lives it had
been said that Jacob was the handsomer. "Yes, Lord,
those two boys sure are good looking; almost pretty.
Of course Thurston's dark but even so, there's no boy
better looking, except for Jacob. That Jacob is the one.
That creamy skin and them blue eyes and that hair, so
straight with that little bit of curl....It's a shame
Thurston couldn't a been born light. He'd have no
match, then. 'Cause he's the one with the sweet ways.
He's the gentle one. The one with the mind for book
learning..."

In his dreams he was dark and he wanted to be dark. Efua was dark and could have him no other way. She was all that Africa meant to black men and he could only love her if he was Kwame and worthy of her. He told himself that he was outgrowing the Tree.

That was why he could see himself as he really was. Surely that was why.

He lay sweating in his sleep, his eyes cast toward the uppermost branches of the tree. Efua came to him and moved her hand gently across his face.

"No," he said. "No, it won't do now. I'm not right anymore." He began screaming." "I've changed. I'm not black enough." His words came in a rush. He turned his head away and felt hot tears rolling down the side of his nose, salty into his mouth.

"You are wrong," she whispered, cradling him in her arms. "You are of my people as I am of my people. It is more than color. It is your history, all of your history which makes you a black man. You are Kwame as he might have been.... Don't throw me away. Don't leave me here."

"No! No," he screamed at her and pushed her away. "It won't work. Don't you see me for what I am. It won't work anymore." He shuddered out of his dream and felt the damp muslin bedsheet between his fingers. He had ripped the botton sheet clear from the bed and was holding it over his private parts like he was ashamed.

Never again could he find Efua or the Sizing Tree in his dreams. Never again was he sure that looking white was an advantage. He would agonize over his loss for the remainder of his life, gradually growing convinced that blackness was somehow an affliction because it was easier to think of it that way.

Jacob sat forward in the chair, confused. The lantern was out and he could smell the taste of whiskey gone sour on his breath. It took him most of the day to recover, and well into the next night, little Nora Evers was born.

Part IV

There were three wick lamps burning high, churning butterfly flickers of light across the ceiling from all the movement in the room. The pain, rhythmic and old, swelled and faded as her bones parted and came together beneath her skin. She thought of her sons, Lawrence and Hamilton, three and a half years in the world; twins like Thurston and Jacob but more alike in their coloring. They were sweet boys and excited about the possibility of having a little sister. She thought of Peter, the youngest, born a year and a half ago, small and frail and frightened in his look. She sensed that she would not see them grown.

"Bear down, Miz Evers." Mrs. Wilks was a brown shadow among the yellow staining lamps, and as shiney. She was waiting at the foot of the bed. Sara's sister, Jennifer, had a damp cloth and was pressing it against the sweat pouring from her face. Jennie was yellow, glowing yellow and shiney like rain and lamp light were pouring over her.

"Oh, Jesus, something in me is tearing loose. The baby is taking me." Sara whispered to herself, afraid to cry out. She had never cried out loud. In all of her life she had been too careful about not making noise. "Lord, I couldn't trust myself to all that strangeness. Please don't let me go before this baby comes." No one heard her. No one answered.

"It's gonna come anytime now, Miz Evers, and then you can rest. Bear down."

Sara pressed and bore down as the bones spread wider and clenched in and ached and opened wider like they would fling the pit of her nakedness open forever.

"Jennie, hold me! Jacob!" Sara screamed from the bottom of her soul and gripped the bed where it was wet from her sweating. A wave of joy passed over her as the baby's head then its shoulders cleared the opening and the small body followed out between her legs, a living slippery mass. The pain subsided as suddenly as it had begun, leaving her weary and jubilant.

"It's a girl, Miz Evers. You got a fine baby girl." Mrs. Wilks' voice reached her from far away and made her laugh. She laughed and tried to raise up off of the pillow, not quite finding the strength.

The room took on the color of day. Always before Sara had felt fine by the third morning or the fourth, but she was hot and weak now and five days had passed in Nora's life. Fever roamed over her and made her teeth chatter at the slightest touch of the air. She shook violently and no one could comfort her. Pain burned a hot wretchedness in her bowels like there was poison in her that somebody had set to boiling.

Why should she have to pay so heavily? Always in her living she had asked questions which no one would answer. Why were so many doors shut? Why was the light fading in the brightest part of a winter day? Why were there so many rules to follow? Why didn't Mrs. Wilks know enough to know that not enough of the afterbirth had been born out of her? Oh Nora, I so wanted to hold you at my breast, to touch you. To see you grow. I'm too weak even to feed you. Some other woman, someone not of your flesh who won't care as much, will hold you. Terror came across her consciousness and froze her into a knot balled up tightly in the bed. A dress shop would have been good for her; something all her own like nothing she had ever had. She heard her dead mother's voice.

"Sara, girl. Come here now and listen to your momma. Now, good little girls don't climb trees. Good little girls keep their dresses down and neat and they walk like ladies."

She had to tell Nora to be a free thing. To blow with the wind the way she had wanted to. Not to hold herself so tightly from life. To climb all the trees and to wrestle hard with the boys for as long as she could win. She had to tell Nora not to answer life as she had answered; weakly saying so many times,

"But Ma. . . .Ma. Let me, please let me. Jacob, don't you think I could. . . .Couldn't we figure a way. . . ."

It seemed to her that all of the fires in the house were going out, one, by one, until a final chilling darkness closed.

a child

boots

Peter, at a little over six years and six months old, lead her for the first time down into the great valley of the branch. It seemed deep, vast and forbidden and drew them to it as secret places do. The water flowed clear liquid satin over the rocks along its bed and bubbled in twists here and there between the bushes and grass like miracles. The sun bathed all the low lying green things, jumbled vines of fox grapes, honey suckle and vetch, and lost itself in oak, cedar, willow and sycamore leaves too thick to share the light with the woods' ground. There was a secret way down a gentle slope of tangled brambles, briars, bird calls and bees, where rabbits sprang and quail shot up from under foot. Nora and Peter thought it was the deepest canyon in the world, field drainage ditch that it was. It was even possible that if they searched awhile, lions and kangaroos might appear from their hidden haunts. Nora sat atop a big rock and watched Peter preparing to launch a leaf boat down the rapids of the branch water. He squated astride the stream at a

point where it was very narrow and aimed the frail
boat toward what he called the open sea. Poppa Jacob
often took him fishing during the summer months and
had explained many times what the open sea was, so
Peter knew very well what he was doing.

Though only five, Nora knew that Peter was beautiful.
His hair was long; way down around his ears and
neck, and it fell heavy and black and shiney and
straight against an olive bronze complexion. His face
was closer to heart shaped than round with gentle
features and black black eyes. When he smiled his
mouth was small, generous and rosey. He was her only
friend. She did not know that she looked much like
him.

One or two years before, Nora had learned that she
had caused her mother's death. Poppa Jacob had told
her several times. She didn't quite know what dying
meant, but she knew it was a terrible thing, and her
birth had caused it. Peter seemed to love her despite
what their father said. "I'm your big brother, Nora,"
he said quite often. "You can come with me anytime
you please and I'll keep you 'tected." Being 'tected
by Peter was an honor she proudly shared with no
one. "Come, now, Nora, you got to make a boat. We
can race 'em all the way from the inlet to the open sea
and then up the river where the water bumps the
rocks and then on past the island and over to the bay.
No need to sail to the ocean today." He knew about
waterways and had even seen the islands which
stretched along the coast between the Eastern Shore
and the Atlantic and made the inland waterway.
"When I'm a sea captain, you can ride with me all
over the world. Get a boat, Nora."

Everybody said Peter talked differently from all of the
other children. Uncle Thurston had taught him to
read and to write when he was only three and there
were books in Uncle's house with charts and hard
words like Pacific and Australia which Peter could

pronounce as easy as you please. It was a wonder.

Nora jumped the long way from the rocktop to the ground and searched for the proper leaf. A large oak leaf was best, just a bit green so it would bend and not so dry that it would soak water and sink. It had to have all of its corners so that they could fold upward toward a small Y-ended stick which had to be placed in the middle for balance. The sail had to be a much smaller oak leaf, pierced by the stick into position so the breeze could give a ride.

"Can't find nothin'," She said.

"OK, take mine." Peter was a true ship builder. He quickly fashioned another fine boat and together, they hung over the water where it spurted past the narrows.

"One, two - go!" and off the boats went, rushing along and turning spirals, sliding bow and stern fast and true toward the tumble rocks. Nora jumped up and down - "Go on ole boat" cheering and screeching her boat toward victory.

The boats were much too frail to withstand the five inch plunge over the last rock in the channel. Both leaves, Nora's leading slightly, flipped over the edge and filled with water.

"Shoot," Nora said, shaking her head. "Boats drown-ded." Peter clicked his teeth with disappointment. He had just learned to do that so he clicked again, rather pleased with the way it sounded.

"Wanta do it again?"

"Nope," Nora yawned. She had been up since dawn and was hungry and sleepy.

"Le's go home, Petey."

"Race you." She couldn't resist. Running was the best thing. They scrambled across the branch, wetting their bare feet and legs, and up the long steep slope of the branch valley toward the open field, dodging branches and each other as they struggled to pass on the narrow foot path. It was impossible not to giggle as they went, each one feeling a chill between the shoulder blades at the thrilling effort to win the race. Peter cleared the woods first, but fell over a particularly deep plow furrow in the new field. Nora pumped her legs and streaked by him, giggling and screaming uncontrolably as she felt him catching up. The way wasn't long to the walnut tree near the house porch and for a second they were even. But Peter was older and stronger and the second passed. He was winning by a yard or two and gaining when old Boots came barking at a gallop out from under the house. Boots was an Irish Setter, long since disabled in the eyes and nose. His old bones hurled at the children as fast as he could haul himself, right into their paths.

The children stopped short, out of breath and just a little frightened as Boots barked like crazy and held them at bay. When he didn't know what he was doing, Boots was known to bite. "Look at ol' Boots barking at us," Nora said. "He mus' think we some little ol' coloured chillun."

"Get on, Boots," Peter shouted, puffing from the exertion. Boots stopped barking and came closer and his tail began to wag. He suddenly stretched and yawned and promptly went back to his bed under the house.

We *are* coloured children," Peter said, shaking his head at Boots and wiping sweat from his face. "Boots just didn't know us. I saw him bark at Poppa the same way a week ago."

"We ain't no coloured chillun."

"Yes we are."

"No, we ain't neither. Tha's not so."

"We are, Nora. Ask Poppa. Come on. Let's go play on the hay stack." He turned and headed for the barnyard.

Nora looked puzzled. Her forehead wrinkled and she wiped the back of her hand across her mouth and then stared blankly. Remebering how the white children, who looked not much different from her and Peter, out at the gate at the end of her father's field had laughed one day and thrown rocks at the dark coloured boy they caught coming by. They hurt him while she stood frightened and looked from one white face to the other, wondering what the boy had done. The boy stood his ground for a few seconds and then turned to run. He stumbled and came close to falling. If he had lost his footing....the rocks they were throwing were large. If he had fallen....Nora had run away and hidden in the barn, she was so frightened by what she saw. The only other time she could remember which made her heart race that way and made her sweat and feel weak all over was when Poppa Jacob had told her about how she had killed her mother. He had shouted at the top of his voice, "Don't you ever touch your mother's picture again. That's the only likeness of her I've got left in this world. You get out, and don't come into this room again. You did enough to her. You killed her as sure as you're standing there. Because of you she'll never come back. Do you hear me? *Do you hear me?*" Nora could still hear her father's voice screaming some nights, and she woke up sweating and scared. Peter always came to her. He would come to her bed and hold her, and once in awhile, when her shaking wouldn't stop, he would let her lie beside him in his bed and she would fall asleep in his arms.

Her brother had never lied to her, but surely he was telling a fib now. Or, he was teasing. That was it.

Nora ran after Peter.

"Petey, You fibbin'? Why you fibbin'?"

"What?"

"We not no coloured chillun! You Fibbin'!"

Peter saw the strickened look on Nora's face and was about to answer when Miss Lottie, their stepmother, stuck her head out of the porch door and called, "Pete, Larry, Hamp, Nora, come get your dinner."

Peter took Nora's hand and headed for the porch, but Nora jerked her hand loose. As he turned around to scold her, she headed at a run back across the field toward the valley. He knew she was hungry and due for a nap. Nora didn't eat right, and the food Miss Lottie cooked tasted awful. Nora was much too skinney and had stomach aches a lot. The smallest thing made her cry, and this was no small thing. She almost never ran away from him, no matter what was wrong.

"I'll be back, Miss Lottie."

"Peter, Peter," Miss Lottie shouted. "You get your tail back in here or you'll get nothing to eat. You hear?"

"I hear," And he went off running, kicking up little clumps of moist dirt as he hurried across the field after his sister, knowing instinctively, as young as he was, that she was in need of comforting. It had happened to him just as suddenly some two years before. Like being hit in the head. Thinking all of his life that he and his family were white folks....

beanie

She was standing in front of Cheriton's only hardware and general merchandise store, a lone little black girl peering into a well dressed window, when Turner Allen came over to her. Field dust covered Beanie Watson from headrag to earth smudged dress to blue jeans and sneakers.

"Hello, Beanie," Turner said walking up to her.

Beanie looked back at him, her dark brown face showing surprise and shyness.

"Hi, Mr. Allen"

"What you doing?"

"Jest looking. Gonna buy me that doll next Saturday." She turned eagerly toward the window. Turner glanced at the dolls. There were several, all of them white with blond hair except one. He was surprised and pleased to see a black doll. They were pretty rarely seen in Cheriton, but maybe the Supreme Court decision would make a difference in a year or so. Things did seem to be changing. The black doll resembled the others in features, but its coloring was dark like his own, a rich brown with black hair.

"You know, that doll's almost as pretty as you." Beanie grinned. Turner added, "And I like that blue dress."

"That's not the one. I wants that one." She pointed to a large blonde doll in a yellow dress. Turner sighed and unconsciously pursed his lips.

"I don't like that one as well," he said. "Now that blue dressed doll looks just like you. It's the most beautiful doll in the window."

Beanie frowned. "I want the white doll. It's the pretty one. Like the one at school."

Turner tried again, feeling an old bitterness in the back of his throat. "If I were buying I'd get the black doll. Anybody can have a white doll these days, but black dolls are rare and they'll always be special."

Beanie laughed. "You a man. You don't buy no dolls." Turner laughed too, sadness hidden underneath. "There's nothing wrong with boys playing with dolls" he said. "They grow up to be fathers, so it's ok to get some practice when they're younger. I owned a doll when I was a boy. People made fun, but I got over the teasing because I enjoyed playing with dolls. They didn't make black dolls then or I would have owned one sure."

Beanie's mouth was hanging just a little open. "You had a doll?" She laughed, still not believing. She couldn't imagine Mr. Turner Allen playing with dolls. Boys weren't supposed to.

"Promise to think about getting that black doll. You give your word?" She nodded her head, agreeing.

"Give me five." Turner reached out his hand and she shook it. He winked. "I'll be seeing you."

"Bye." He walked away, a great big tall coloured man. Seemed like everybody looked up to him. His car was a Cadillac. His house was the prettiest and biggest coloured folks' house in Cheriton; in the whole county, and just as fine as the fine white folks' houses. Folks believed in him because he kept his word, he had finished college and he wasn't uppity, and he talked plainly and there was something powerful about him. She knew this. Grown people she knew spoke well of him often. His words were not to be taken lightly.

Sometimes she was jealous of his daughter, Carrie, for having such a father as Mr. Allen. Beanie wondered where *her* Daddy was. She had heard so many stories about where missing father's might be that she was afraid to ask her mother, and her mother didn't like to talk about him. Some kids said their daddies had run off. Beanie didn't want to hear that about her own. But it was hard not to ask. Her mother just said once or twice that she missed him and loved him and he was gone to the Lord's Place. Beanie wasn't sure where that was, but she suspected. Didn't want to know. The two dolls stood side by side, one in yellow, one in blue. One like the strangers. One like her. One white and one black. They were the same price; nine-ninety-five. She groaned. Mr. Allen was an important man and a wise man according to the preacher and when he said something it was usually the wise thing to listen and to heed him. Maybe she'd ask her mother. Maybe the black doll was better.

Beanie ran into the store. Sara was just finishing her business; making the last payment on a kerosene lamp and some coal oil. Sara looked tired and walked the same. She had worked in the fields all week from sun to sun. Now she looked hot and bothered.

Beanie tugged at her dress.

"Let's go, baby," Sara said. "Everythin' costs so

much. Lord if I knows where the ends is gonna come together." She took Beanie by the hand and started out of the store. Beanie figured her mother had too much on her mind to worry over a doll so she didn't say anything. Maybe later. The maybe stuck in her mind and made her restless and strangely afraid.

Beanie had wanted a doll from the time she was five, but she was broke until she turned seven and could work regularly. It had taken over two years to save enough. She traded in old pop bottles for deposit money when she was lucky enough to find them, and a store man down the way from her house bought scrap metal that she scavenged for a few pennies a pound. Her allowance was usually five cents a week during field picking season, but sometimes she only received a penny. Even when she made all of sixty-cents in a day, she could only keep a nickle or maybe half of that at the end of the week. Food and clothes and school and the doctor man took the rest. But now she had enough and the doll filled her dreams even in the soundest sleep.

Six mornings after her talk with Turner Allen she awoke well before light and watched as the world outside of her house recovered its familiar looks from the darkness. Green things were almost gray where the first traces of the day's sun began playing on drops of dew and reflected the whispy morning clouds. She watched the coming day and her eyes grew wide with wonder. There always seemed some mystery. From the first gray, way in the earth's corners, the reds and oranges to pinks were now on the glide up over the trees over yonder. From where she was it looked like the sun was rising out of Mr. Jacob's chimney, puffing smoke as it came. The rising spread and like some invisible thief, it stole all traces of night away and the morning was again, ordinary.

Beanie ran around to the back of the house. She pulled three of the foundation bricks away, reached in

through the hole and pulled out an old Maxwell
House coffee can. The can rattled with coins. Beanie
shook it and laughed just listening. She saw her
father, a man not tall, not short, brown she knew or
she figured, brave she hoped and young like her
Momma was sometimes. She saw happiness in all
kinds of shapes. She closed her eyes and shook the can
vigorously, listening to the music of the metalic rattle.
She wanted to count it again to make sure all of the
money was there, but before she could get the lid off,
she heard Mr. Robin's truck coming down the field
road. So she put the can back in its place, giving it a
love pat before she reached for the bricks. Tomorrow
was the buying day and she had decided without her
mother's help. She would trust Mr. Allen and leave
Cheriton with the black doll in her arms.

The folk on the truck kept talking and gossiping while
staring out over the land. Before long they were
stretched out among the stringbean rows which waved
green and squat to the ground in the field. Some folks
worked along the rows with their knees deep in the
powdery dry earth while others preferred to stand bent
over. It took a lot of picking to fill a bushel basket
with snap beans. Beanie worked fast, but by noon she
only had a couple of baskets full.

They ate under a willow tree. Folks were everywhere,
lying still and stretching out kinks. Beanie didn't
mean to, but she fell asleep with half of her sandwich
still in her hand.

Sara removed the sandwich and folded it away into
waxed paper. Maybe Beanie could eat it later in the
day. Sara shook her head slowly, so that she felt the
mood of the movement inside of her where she was
frightened. It was worse in the middle of the night
when the wind breezed by her despite closed windows
and she was alone with the winter cold and the
darkness. She saw herself reflected someplace one day.
Some white lady's mirror or maybe it was a pane of

store glass. She didn't know who the woman was for a second because in her mind's eye she looked the same as when she was eighteen. Now so shabby and strange. What husband would she ever find to want her. What good man. Her hands stained with picking things and wrinkled right hard from scrubbing in hot water and water half froze. She would always be alone. There were lots of no accounts who would gladly take up space, but no good man, one who could take care of her and Beanie, was going to come along. They were already took. She thought of her Al and their loving buried with him in the ashes of his Florida grave. Nobody to help her feed Beanie. Nobody to even come to the grave when she put them down; Al and baby Willie burned to cinders. Just some strange undertaker with a little dust between his fingers and the local preacher man and the smell of smoke still in her clothes and hair.

"Oh, Lord," Sara sighed. "I wishes so much she didn't have to miss her schooling." She thought on, talking silently in her head and counting without numbers the rises and falls of her daughter's breathing. It was as much a clock of time as any made of faces and hands. The in and out of Beanie's life was more out of breath than full of fresh air. Sara moaned, thinking for a moment that Beanie was older now than when they left the field to eat lunch. So old that she looked like Sara's mother lying there. The apparition dissolved and again, Beanie was nine years old.

Sara wiped the strain and sweat from her face and pulled at a clump of pine grass nearby. Folk were moving back to their labor. Back into the green of it, the long bean thin of it. The aching of it. She never could stand field work. Lordy. She never could stand it no way.

She decided to let Beanie sleep under the willow. It was pleasant to steal a nap. She remembered the rare

times when she was a little thing and her mother had
let her sleep longer than expected.

"Lie you down and sleep my chil'.
Lie you down and rest.
When you wake from sleep my chil';
Things will be better by and by.

"Let me rock away your fears.
Momma here to guard you.
Let me rock away your tears
Things will be better by and by."

Sara's voice was far from fine but it held a sweetness
and much feeling. The melody was old and haunting.
She finished a verse and tucked the blanket into the
mattress. It had been a long day for Beanie, even with
her sleeping away part of the afternoon. Right after
supper, with her mind set on tomorrow's trip to
Cheriton and the doll, Beanie had taken herself to
bed, hoping the night would pass quickly.

"Lie you down and hold your faith.
Good things coming one day.
Lie you down and hug your doll.
Momma found it far away."

Sara reached under the bed where she had hidden the
new doll. She had gone to Cheriton special two days
ago while Beanie was still in the school house. Beanie
had told her weeks ago which one she wanted; the one
with the yellow dress. Sara laid it quietly in Beanie's
arms, whispering her prayers for Beanie's happiness
softly into the night, and sat back in her rocker. The
paleness of the doll was almost lost against the sheet.
Sara smiled, satisfied, not knowing the change made,
singing,

"Lie you down and sleep my chil'.
Lie you down and say,

Everything is gonna be fine
Because tomorrow is a brand new day."

to struggle

thickets

"Williams. Private Harry Williams. You and Curlie and Jones. Patrol.

"Yas, suh, Lieutenant. Sheeit!"

Like a recording the man said, "This village is secure. This patrol's purpose is to reconnoiter the thickets immediately adjacent to the village perimeter for any sign of VC. Now shake the lead out. Move it out."

Charlie wants me to hunt charley for him. "Tch, huh. Yas Suh, Lieutenant. Sheeit."

There were three brothers ahead of me and I could see at least two hunkies behind. It was a small patrol. In all of my days of toting a gun through bushes, hunting rabbit, quail, squirrel, deer, I had never seen woods so thick. There was a reluctance in me for which I had no words. I could taste it like a sour belch lingering on my breath. It wasn't just a fear of being attacked and maybe dying or being maimed. I was afraid of the very idea of hunting people, and I knew the white boy, Billy, directly behind me, wasn't far removed from hunting me and all of my folk back stateside. It was no secret that he hated black men, and had even told some Vietnamese women that all brothers had long monkey like tails and something akin to baseball bats in their pants. Billy was real scared now. Every other step his fright shot out of his mouth. "What's that? You hear something?" Every man on the patrol had VC popping out of his pores thanks to Billy, but he kept it up.

"Shut up, Billy" the Corporal said finally, "Shut your damn mouth." Billy had me so jumpy I was scared I might shoot myself. Lord have mercy. His fear was in all of us. Nobody needed reminding.

"Hey, Harry. What we gonna do if they jump out of these bushes? Harry?"

"Shut up, Billy. Shhh ...."

Curlie stepped out of line, let me and Billy pass and then grabbed Billy from behind. "Hush up mother fucker or you gone get my boot up your asshole"

"Git off me, nigger." I turned on Billy, too, intent on accidentily spreading his teeth. The bushes moved ahead of us and Billy screamed.

"Lord. VC! VC!"

I wheeled about. My foot caught in a vine and as I went down on my knees I saw a blur of black pajamas and a shock of dark hair under a wide straw-woven hat.

The enemy screamed and raised his hands to his mouth. In that second he looked directly into my face. But I was committed, my finger already squeezing in.

Blacks pajamas and a shock of dark hair. The bullets picked him up off of the ground and flung him backwards like a floating kite caught by a hard chunked brick. The hat fell away and the hair fell long around the enemy's shoulders as the body came to rest in a patch of high grass.

I dropped my gun. Billy touched my shoulder. I hit him, punched him, jammed my knee into his balls and left him crying on the ground.

She seemed a child. I had broken her ribs. Her lungs were laid open like bread. My gun had severed her right arm at the shoulder so that it was totally gone. The medic came.

She stared into my face, her mouth open and blood coming in a slow foam across her tongue. The fresh raw odor of her dying clouded my face. I ran my tongue over my lips, expecting to taste my own blood there. Very brown. I couldn't seem to see anything else except that she was brown like me. Her eyes were black and my hand against her skin was the same shade of brown. Vomit gushed into my mouth. I fought for breath like a drowning man, gaging, forcing the stuff back down inside of me. I sounded strange to myself, like someone over my shoulder was vomiting with his mouth closed. Her eyes were the deepest black I had ever seen until they glazed over.

The Corporal came over to me where I was sitting on the ground. He lit a cigarette and put it between my lips like we were in some John Wayne flick about the French Foreign Legion. "Nice work, Private," he said. The cigarette fell to the ground and I moved away from him and the sight of the girl. I felt sick and sat down again. The white soldier inched closer, remained standing and talked down to me. "You never can tell about these people," he said. "She was probably VC."

"Naw, man" I mumbled to myself. "A girl. Just a girl. A little girl...."

"Ah, come on, Williams," he said. "You done right. May even get a medal."

I looked up into his face. "Ah shit, git away from me, man."

The Corporal coughed. "I - I don't like to do this, Williams," he said, "but, well, I'll have to put you on report for Billy. For hitting Billy. You know."

the real
hidden meaning
of undertaking

The sheriff was a rather handsome man. He didn't look anything like a policeman when he wasn't dressed in his uniform. Of course, that was seldom the case. Some folks said he'd been poured into his uniform, he wore the khaki clothes with the brown leg stripe so much. When he wore his gun his eyes were hard and dry ice cold. His mouth became a straight line when he wore the gun and pinned on the badge and hung the nightstick from his great big leather belt. He entered Turner's office and refused to sit down. All the time they talked he walked around the room, looking at the pictures and academic degrees framed on the office walls: Hampton Institute, St. Paul's, Eckles Embalming School, Morgan State. The sheriff's manner was deceivingly casual and his words slipped from between his teeth in a slow southern way. An observer might have thought that Luke had never been in Turner's office before.

"I spoke with Logun, Turner," the sheriff said. Turner sat in his desk chair, listening, his feet crossed and resting on a low foot stool.

"He's assured me he won't bother you all, so you'd best drop your charges against him. You won't git a charge to stick against a white man. Not in Northampton County you won't."

Turner gazed steadily at Luke as the peace officer moved from picture to diploma around the room.

"You know, he's right decent," Luke continued. "I mean, Logun's willing to let things simmer down. But if you press your complaint, I can't guarantee he'll take it peaceable. No man likes being threatened. And no white man's gonna take threatenin' from a nigger."

"How about threats from the law?" Turner said, ignoring Luke's pet name for him.

Luke puckered his mouth and smiled. "Well, this here thing about law is a matter of how you're standing."

Turner smiled and shook his head as he looked down at his desk. A chill of anger passed over him causing the hair to rise along his arms and down his back.

"Now, when it comes to it, your daughter was unlawful to hit the Green boy."

"He was yelling lewd words at her."

"As I was saying, Mr. Green ain't pressing no charges against your girl for hitting his son. Them folk is being more'n decent if you ask me. You go on now and think about this thing."

Luke paused and looked down at the shiney steel and wooden handle of his pistol. "I strongly advise you not to ride Logun any further, boy, 'cause if you do, Lord. He ain't very big but he can be mean as death when he hankers to."

Turner stared through the sheriff. His anger was a living thing with a heartbeat much steadier than his own and a heart more demanding. He sat there, feeling his anger, and heard his voice reaching back deep into the thoughts he must finally say.

"Do you know what it is to meet death, Luke?"

Luke did a slow double take, his right hand closing firmly around the pistol butt as he heard what he heard. His mouth dropped partly open and remained there, uncertain of what it would do next.

"I've been an undertaker for sixteen years," Turner said. "I've taken the blood from over 2600 black peple in that time and traded it for embalming fluid. We know how to die, Luke, and we meet old man death all the time. But every so often I get to see something rather strange about our dying. It's not that we're afraid of dying or afraid of fighting to live, but it's as if we're afraid that dying by a white hand for breaking a white neck will be harder or more terrible or something like that. In a way that's true. We haven't had much power to protect our own. But it comes off like a white man's life is worth more." Turner looked Luke in the eye and smiled. "Why don't you sit down, Sheriff. Take a load off your feet."

Luke was stunned. He'd been caught open. His mind couldn't seem to click over fast enough to encompass the arrogance of Turner's speech. "I think you'd best shut your mouth, Turner."

"No. Listen a little longer, Luke." Turner's eyes narrowed. "I want you to understand something."

"It seems to me you've said enough," Luke said, stepping closer. Anger and a strange unaccustomed fear tinted his voice. He was being challenged by a nigger. Such a thing had never happened to him before. No. It had happened once or twice, but the circumstances were better and all he had to do was shoot. All those niggers had been poor. "I asked you a question, Luke, Do you know what it is to meet death?" "Listen, Turner...."

Their eyes met, sliced at one another, reached out and held on hard. Turner saw the fear in Luke's eyes and made note of it. The dynamics of an old childhood personality struggle had set the room to a sizzling silence. Even as a kid Turner had been able to subdue Luke. It had been that way in every fight they had ever had, and when Luke and his friends ganged up on Turner, there were always Turner's brothers.

Luke switched the weight of his stance from one hip to the other, poised and undecided whether to leave or to kill Turner right there. A rage was coming on. Arrogant nigger. If Turner was begging to be shot, Luke figured he'd stay and listen and confirm, or so he told himself.

"I might have killed a *black* man yesterday if he'd done what Logun did, Luke. That Green boy taunted my daughter and called her dirty names and she hit him. He's been teasing her, calling her nigger, for months. It was between them. Logun's a grown man. He had no cause to intervene the way he did. When he laid hands on my children for telling off that boy he laid hands on me. Killing Logun seemed to mean more than killing a black man, though. And that's the way the law is set. Now, I thought about that thing. And I've decided that this over-value on white life has got to be reduced to something ordinary. If a white man's not worth shit and fucks with me, he's got to be buried in a deep hole."

Luke undid the trigger guard of his holster. A sickening uneasiness passed over him. The movement was a defensive reflex, used many a time before and intended to intimidate. Luke wasn't quite ready to take on this kind of murder; at least not in Turner's office. On the other hand, he *was* the sheriff. He could probably get by.

"Luke, you tell Logun I've decided I'm ready to outlive him. Tell him if he's not ready to die, he'd best stay away from us. And the charges against him will stand. No matter how crooked that court, at least we'll take it that far."

Luke's coloring flushed a deeper red. He remained poised, his hand near his gun, like someone had turned him off in midstride. A kind of shock had him; a kind of embarrassed insecurity showed plainly on his face and filled him up to his eyes.

"I've got a passel of brothers," Turner continued. "I talked to them last night. You remember my brothers, don't you, Luke? Tell Logun if he or any peckerwood white ass lays a finger on me, my brothers will have more than enough money to hunt him down. There's no place they won't go and no place you and Logun can hide."

Luke moved in an angry rush across the room toward Turner. He leaned forward over the desk and spat saliva and words into Turner's face. "Nigger, who do you think you're fooling with your Jesus talk. You forgetting I'm a white man or something. You and all the niggers in China betta get one thing straight. You don't threaten me. You damn well don't threaten me."

Turner smiled again. "Luke, we've got the power, right here, now. It's taken a long time, but it's here. between me and my brothers who live in so many different places you couldn't begin to find them all. I think you'd best go." Turner's voice was tight and low.

"God damn you! I come here to help you boy. You don't have the sense to know when you're well off."

Luke swung his flat hand toward Turner's face. Turner caught his arm at the wrist. Their faces were almost touching as Turner held Luke tight. Luke returned Turner's stare as steadily as he could, but the look on Turner's face and the intensity of his eyes worked like fire until the sheriff's face was beet red again and he had to look away. He snatched his hand back, all of him one gesture of rage.

"This isn't over, nigger. This damn well isn't over." Luke turned and started for the door. "You'd best watch every move you make, nigger. Watch your wife and your children. Nobody talks to me the way you've talked tonight."

"If you come back here meaning me harm be ready to die, Luke. Bring a shovel for your remains and be ready to die. I'm holding you responsible for my good health and as sure as you're born, you won't live more than a week if you lay a hand on me or mine. You know how torturous my brothers can be, Luke. In fact, I'm sure you remember." Luke's hand went involuntarily to his neck. There was a scar there, beneath his collar. A rope burn left there by a large family of niggers long ago when he was much younger.

The door slammed and Turner Allen opened his mouth and took in air. The room seemed to move before his eyes for a moment as he blinked and held his head back to ease the tension in his neck. The 45 on the desk shelf by his knee looked unreal and when he picked it up it felt like flesh gone to sleep for all time. He laid the gun down on his desk and gripped his knees to stop the shaking. His whole body was trembling. Things would be even worse now, maybe. But he had done what he had to do and he was satisfied. He had walked too many bridges in the last few hours to deny himself the other side now. Luke's judgment day and the judgment day of his kind was coming, and every black man, every woman of colour in the world, would be the undertaker on that day, each with earth to sprinkle at the order and the chant.

the grief

It was amazing how the night fell on the house on that
evening, overcoming it in a gulf of darkness so sudden
that he thought the old logs; so long ago pegged and
wedged into place by his people under the whip, would
splinter beneath the invisible pressure, crushing him
inside with all of the trappings of his bondage. He had
never imagined that any place could be as strange and
void of humane considerations and as frightening as
the new world. Nothing like his home and its pieces of
understanding, which any intelligent man or woman
could lay into place. (...the running of the waters the
changing colors of time the growth of vegetation the
manners of people, their duties and wanton acts
making the village hum with things definable even to
the deaf and blind the faces of days the sweetness of
even galling enemy besieged nights the sounds of the
gods in his children the speeches of birds the tastes of
sustenance his wife's laughter. All that, home, and
far away; waiting, yet gone.....)

He had been taught by his father that if a man hurt enough to cry, he should do so, wherever he was. So now, finally quieted by the first spiritual exhaustion he had ever known and despite the continuing rage of twelve vaccuous months of slavery and exile; chained to a wall at his ankles, manicled wrist to wrist, his vision of night through the storage house window gridded by iron bars, Musiemi cried.

The boy watched him; had been watching him since before sunset, because his master desired it. He had never imagined that a black man of Musiemi's stature existed in the world. A black man whose eyes could not seem to look down; whose back stayed straight; whose voice was never heard to speak English despite whippings and beatings and angry commands by Marse Blanche and his three sons. He had cost more than any slave ever bought as best the boy knew. Whipping him was as foolish and as wasteful as burning one's own house when there was no insurance. It seemed that even Marse Blanche didn't dare do but so much, he had already paid so high. Musiemi had become master despite slavery and chains. All of this had had a profound effect upon Young. He had been on the verge of believing in Musiemi, until tonight when he saw the man crying. A man wasn't supposed to do that. Not a proud strong, master of a man.

Young turned away from Musiemi in disappointment, not understanding the ancient freedom given the man by his culture. He laid down on a straw mat in the fartherest corner and felt disgust.

Musiemi, deep in his grief, catching a breath from all of the agony of his bitterness, sensed the change in Young. He turned, clanking his chains and spoke in an African tongue, fluid and resonant, asking what the trouble was; why it was that Young's eyes weren't on him as they had been for so many weeks now.

Young, who understood only the pidgeon English taught him by Marse Blanche, sat on his elbow in surprise. It was the first time that Musiemi had spoken to him. He decided to get his disgust off his chest even though he assumed that Musiemi would not understand him.

"What you crying like that for?"

Musiemi smiled sadly and eased himself within the weight of his chains into a sitting position on the damp earthen floor. He understood. Languages came easily to him and he had heard enough English in a year to know the meanings of many things. He answered in Kamba, "Because I am a man and I am in pain, here, where my feelings originate. All that is beautiful and precious has been taken from me except my anger, and it has yet to learn the patience for cunning. A man who cannot use his body as it was designed for use is one who falsifies his reality. My eyes can make water as the heavens and my bladder can. And as in drought and times of great inner accumulation, I would empty my eyes and drain my heart. Little boy, you slave maker's watch dog, I could pee this place into oblivion. But first I must make you a black man and take your thoughts home. Your mind is as white and as cold as the snows of the late winter." Young did not understand.

Nor would he ever. Three days later, his heart finally too far gone to grief to withstand another hour of bondage, Musiemi was shot dead while escaping. Young, only a black slave boy and known by his master to be so devoted that he was allowed access to the plantation armory, was not punished further for shooting the valuable, but intractable Musiemi down.

and to die

november

On one particularly cold November evening when I was eight years old, I walked into my father's morgue, pulled a chair up beside the embalming table, climbed upon it so that my head was almost the height of his, and watched as he methodically snipped away with scissors and scalpel at the entrails of a man who had blown himself into death, by accident, while hunting rabbits with a twelve-gauge shotgun. I had seen dead men in blood before. The shock of seeing was always subtle and cold near the base of my breast bone. I could never prepare for it, though from my father's reaction to me, the shock never showed. My mind and throat knew it well. It felt like being caught at smoking cigarettes behind the house after making sure that no one, especially my father, was within a mile. It felt like trying to eat dinner before the whipping in my room. It took hold of me like the anger and disappointment in his eyes across the food, when I was wrong and caught and about to answer.

Tears formed in the corners of my eyes as I looked at the dead man. I pretended to cough and wiped them away.

The dead man had a beautiful body. His complexion was brown-black and he would have been tall had he been standing. His shoulders and chest were broad and heavily muscled and tapered to a waist blue-gray and ragged with power burns and mangled pieces of flesh. For some reason there was a piece of cloth over his face and neck, and he was covered with a surgical sheet from his pelvis down to his toes.

I didn't know who he was. An hour before, while playing with three friends, the hearse had passed us, headed home. I played another half hour or so, giving my father enough time to unload the body and prepare it for embalming, and then I hurried home to watch. Over the last year I had gradually worked my way up to observing the whole procedure. Most were simple operations. The odor still bothered me, but I was gradually getting used to it.

Daddy's transparent surgical gloves, the brown of his hands showing through, were covered with a thin film of the dead man's blood. The explosion had ripped his mid-section to pieces. His circulatory system was so badly damaged that he would quickly rot and smell if all of his insides weren't removed. I watched and held my breath and frowned, almost bringing my face to pain.

Daddy opened a large plastic bag and slowly began placing the tangle of intestines and organs into it. The room filled with the strong odor of a gutted chicken, subdued only by the stronger odor of the embalming fluid. Its vapors watered my eyes.

"Are you sure you want to watch this?" Daddy said. "This is the first time you've seen a bad case like this one, you know."

"I don't know. It's alright, Daddy," I swallowed hard and gritted my teeth.

He smiled. "Yes it's alright, but it's awful." He stopped working and looked at me. "Why don't you go back into the fresh air. You can't learn anatomy in one day. You're rather young to try."

I smiled to reassure him. "I'm okay." I wanted to stay. I wanted to be a doctor one day. There was a lot to learn.

"Well, take your coat off, then. We'll be here awhile."

I put my coat on another chair and returned to my place. "How did he die?"

"A witness said he propped his gun against his side while lighting a cigarette and the gun went off."

"Who was the witness?"

"His father."

"Did his father cry?"

Daddy paused as though he had no answer. After while he said, "Yes, his father cried."

"Can I die?"

Daddy continued working. "Go sit over there for a few minutes," he said. "Give yourself a breather."

I jumped down to the floor and found a seat away from the table. When I was quiet again, he said, "Yes, you can die." I imagined myself dead for a moment. I saw myself lying on the embalming table but I didn't look dead to me.

"My first brother died, didn't he?"

Daddy took a deep breath. "Your brother was stillborn. In a sense, he never lived."

I was quiet for a moment. "It must be funny to die before you live, huh?"

He shook his head just a little and turned on the

embalming pump. The machine hummed and
throbbed and I leaned back against the chair, moving
my fingers to the rhythm of the machine. The
embalming fluid pumped in, the blood spurted out
onto the table in a pulsating flow from tubing placed
into the main vein of the dead man's right armpit,
draining away, and I remembered the look of the wall
paper in my bedroom. The background was a pale,
almost white shade of pink, and tiny figures skating
in pairs were scattered in a pattern around the walls. I
loved to ice skate. Daddy turned the pump off for a
minute and then turned it on again.

On cold days I skated all day, sometimes. The only
pond in the neighborhood was small, and I wasn't
allowed to skate at night. Only white people were
allowed to skate at night. They could skate in the
daytime, too. It was the law, but it seemed strange.
Some nights, when I was supposed to be in bed, I
climbed into the attic and watched the figures skating
before the bonfires. They were lovely to see as they
moved and danced through a sparse growth of
trees. I wanted to skate, watching them. Sometimes I
told myself that I was going to sneak out of the house
one night and go right to them and skate anyway, but
I knew they'd throw me off of the ice. Like they did
Bobby Williams one time. So I never tried. I was
scared.

Chuck Morris showed me a place one time just after a
heavy rain where the water had frozen over a huge
mud hole. He and some of the other kids decided to
skate there after dark. It was some distance beyond
the regular pond in the clearing behind my house. We
built a fire and brought food. It was only big enough
for three skaters at one time, so we took turns. I fell in
love with Chuck that night, but Chuck never knew. He
was too old to know.

After an hour, the ice gave way. It was really too small
and thin to support us. Daddy said he would dig out a

place and fill it with water for us when he had the time. But being the only undertaker in the County, he never got to it. Lots of black folk died in the wintertime. He was just as busy in the summer, but in the summer the weather was too hot and no one thought about ice skating enough to plan ahead.

Daddy had been watching me for several minutes now. He was a big, kind man. Sometimes when he was in the kitchen just before dinner, he had a way of putting his arms around Mamma's waist and hugging her. Whenever he did that he kissed her lightly on the mouth, patted her lightly on her behind and then sat down at the table with a satisfied, mischievous look on his face, the two of them always smiling. Dinner was always especially happy on those occasions. The kitchen seemed warmer.

"Sweetheart, are you alright?"

"Uuhuh. You almost finished?"

"Almost."

He shut the pump off, disconnected the hoses and began suturing the last incision under the man's left arm. The cloth no longer covered the dead man's face. I hadn't noticed Daddy removing it. As I walked toward the table to get a look, Daddy smeared a lubricant over the man's face and hands to keep them soft.

There was suddenly something very familiar about the shape of the still mouth and nose. He wasn't a man. He was a boy; eighteen years old. His belly was sewn together now, sunken and empty. All signs of the blood were gone. Before dressing him, thick wads of newspaper would be placed over his abdomen to pad him out smooth. The public would never know how empty he was.

The light in the room dimmed to me for a moment, and though I wanted to move my feet, they wouldn't move. I heard the dogs running rabbit. I felt the awful gun go off, both barrels point blank against my side.

I ran to the sink and leaned over. All my supper gagged out of me. I choked and gagged and coughed and finally caught my breath, as the feeling went away, and I turned back towards Daddy, numb. He removed his gloves and as I leaned against his waist he wiped my face with a cold, wet towel.

"He's a boy. He's John. He's John, Daddy."

Daddy took me into his arms and carried me outside. My face lay against his shoulder. I looked through my tears behind us as he walked along. The morgue door was so big and white and awesome.

"Carrie, I thought you knew. This is the first time you've lost somebody isn't it?"

"John's dead. He's my friend. He's dead."

He held me closer and moved his hand gently back and forth across my hair as he carried me towards my room. His shirt was soon wet near the collar. I watched the damp place against his shoulder as he pulled the covers up about me and held my hands until the room grew dark and I couldn't hear the dogs running rabbit anymore.

gone after jake

The windshield wipers worked endlessly, gathering futile momentum back and forth across the glass, swishing out a rhythm which echoed shoopa, shoopa over the dashboard, across the back of the rear seat and into the spacious cargo area of the stationwagon where the stretcher rested inert and waiting. The rubber blades swung their way across the glass and bared no space under the falling rain sufficient for him to see much of anything on the road ahead.

Turner clicked his teeth and rubbed the palm of his hand against the fogged windshield. The defroster, on the blink from its winter agonies, was no match for the unseasonable cold.

He was well off the main road. The pitch blackness beyond the car's headlights seemed impenetrable, as though the world through which he navigated was made of tar. So he eased the car along, hoping he wouldn't have to stop and wait it out. It wasn't for him to keep his callers waiting. He could think of no circumstances, except his own death, which would excuse such a failure in the minds of the people in the community. People were waiting for him to take the stench and ache of death from out of their bedrooms and livingrooms and from off their kitchen floors. High tides, snow or heat wave, hurricane blowing; there'd be no forgiving if he didn't get there now. And no forgiving meant a lost account; money lost and a loss of prestige for having failed. He had to get there, and once he arrived, all actions would have to be quiet and smoothly executed and over in a quick finality so that the bedsheets could be burned with the mattress and misery sent out of the windows when the family aired the death room.

Turner grunted impatiently and eased the car along. The water gurgling from the wind blowing up the bottom half of the windows brought things to his mind. He remembered when he was a boy of ten or so, driving a car which had no windshield. When it rained the driver and anyone else on the front seat were a catch-all: Wind, leaves, water and consternation.

Turner blinked his eyes. He was tired and listening absently to himself thinking. Folks he'd known often came and spoke to him when he was lonely and tired and seeking the dead.

"Yes, shoot'em-all-yes, brother. Water falling from heaven on a dead man the day they buries him brings good luck aplenty. You hear me?"

Another voice. Somebody or other standing on the far side of the oil heater at the store down the way. "Shit man. Luck nothing. You try tellin the dead man about some kinda luck."

Talking in the cemetery. Grave diggers talking and digging graves. "Raining. Ain't that what I say. It's the Lord crying 'cause death done struck another blow to one a his coloured childrens."

"Man, look at you. Standing down in that hole with

water filling your boots to your knees and you think the Lord's got time to be messing in your business. If anythang he's taking a leak."

His people theorizing about the rain and dying and laughing death down, scared and digging graves and calling each other niggers while making holes for black men to be covered up in. Bad weather and dying. Too much of that for black folk, and them helping it along. Turner shivered from the cold and backed away from his thoughts. They made him sore inside.

The rain was heavier. The car was rocking like hands had hold of it from either side, pushing and pulling. He checked the field road and almost had to swim through the rain to get back to the stationwagon. Pot-holes aplenty. Mud and ooze and then the hardpacked ground beneath the dirt road that he counted on to keep the tires gripping. The car slipped and slid through the field and held precariously until he drove into Jake's yard. He opened the door and an old fox hound, guarding its hind parts from the gale, stuck its nose out from under the house and howled. The wind was so strong that Turner couldn't even hear the sound. There was just the upraised mouth caught in the light beneath the porch, opening and closing as though the dog was mute.

A hand parted dingy curtains at a window and slid the yellowed shade back. An eye in a dark face stared out at the white funeral car as the headlight beams shut off and the engine died; clicking off its heat under the noise of the storm. The eye seemed to ease across the shade, though it was out of sight, passing in a shadow toward the door. By the time Turner stepped into the house, the old woman was seated, rocking in a chair that cried each time it moved. Except for one dim kerosene lamp near the front window, her face was lighted entirely by the red glow of a pot bellied stove, so that sitting there, moving in and out of the glow, her face took on the ambience of another place from where her body was.

A kettle suddenly whistled a shrill wail. Jake's wife made no move for it. Turner stepped quickly across the room and removed it from the stove. He still had goose flesh, standing there looking down at her, the kettle steaming in his hand, and a feeling of moving among ghosts from the sound it had made.

She rocked and made the crying sound with the chair. "You come to take my husband away, Mr. Allen." She spoke in almost a commanding tone, her voice higher in pitch than he had ever heard it, like the whine of the chair, except her's was human and forlorn.

"Well, you can take him. He wasn't much account. I'm glad he's gone to glory. Yes, Lord. Have mercy, Jesus! I'm glad he's gone. You hear me?"

Mrs. Harris leaned forward, clapped her hands together in a quick soft motion and raised them before her, palms out, fingers straight up and above her head, spread apart. Like Sunday go-to-meeting revival time at the Baptist church down the way; like other black folk from all around, praying and shouting their sinning down; her hands moved beseeching God. "Praise the Lord. God help me, Mr. Allen. Praise the Lord. He wasn't no good. You knows that. You seen him around here." She started up out of the chair, screaming now so that Turner had to rush to hold her.

"I know. I know. Hush now. Won't do no good." He said the words softly over and over, barely hearing himself for listening to her and trying to hold her down. She was stronger than an old woman was supposed to be. "You seen him around here. He was no account." She shouted and tears rolled down and dripped like rain, cold on the back of his neck, while she gripped his shoulders, exerting all of her strength to climb over him. Turner held her in the chair, sometimes looking into her wrinkled black face glowing red and tortured at him in the dark.

"He was tall and straight. Don't you remember, Mrs. Harris. Jake was tall and straight."

"Yes. Yes he was. Tall. I knows that. You gonna say he done his best. You gonna say he worked hard and fed me and the children. I knows that. But he wasn't no account to go and die the way he done. He's left me all by myself, Mr. Allen. He's lying in there all drawed up. Life all shrunk out of him. He didn't even say nothing before he left. Jest went off in his sleep all drawed up." She caught her breath for a second, sighed heavily and then seemed to hold her breath again as if she might keep it locked up indefinitely. The air rasped out of her throat when she spoke again. "Lord, he used to love to eat. Piled his plate high whenever we had the food and he loved it. You remember when he pulled your brother out the swimming hole. Jake was a high pockets man. Hips high on them great long legs. Fine at loving. Course, we ain't been together that way for a great long while. Oh, my, my, my," Her voice ebbed away and she fell back in the chair and shuddered. "He died so hard. And there's nothing in the world familiar to me no kinda way now."

Turner said almost nothing. He didn't know what or how. There was nothing in him. He waited with her until the tension passed from her words and then he carried her to a neighbor's house.

Jake leaned a rhythm when he walked. He walked with a bop, his right ankle always giving way a little just before he put his full weight down. Now, there he was, lying cancerous boney and sunken cheeked on his deathbed, the warm rancid dank odor of his urine all through the room.

As he covered the legs, drawn up tight to Jake's chest from a long rolling agony, covered the stiff still warm old man, brought the sheet towards gray stubbled cheeks and temples, and cut off the light from the aged and misery yellowed eyes, he looked down into the old man's face and saw the missing places, the broken places where those once fine even teeth in better days had ground down on life. The mouth was drawn, ill, tortured. Turner could tell that the storm hadn't abated. It was still going on. Looking down into the open misshappen place where his friend's voice had boomed and whispered, in the center of himself, something tightened in Turner, like it would break apart. He wanted to say something, now, to Jake, futile as it was, knowing there was no need and no way to give comfort to him now and wondering why he had let himself fail the old woman when she was alive now still, and needed desperately to hear something better than his inept silence. Turner strained to say something. Shook his head. The only thing he could think of was, "It's raining, Jake. I'll be sure to cover you from the rain."

the mute

Part I

There was a cricket in the grass beside Peter's basement window, and everytime Cook Laura took a step closer to the house, the cricket did its best to announce her coming.

"Shut up, cricket," Laura whispered under her breath. "You blacker than I is. No need a you telling white folks I'se coming." Laura took three more steps toward the window and peeked around the hedge which ran parallel to that part of the house. The yard was quiet, and the woods beyond. The baying was long over now. Marse Stone had come in around one o'clock, after the killing. If he had been drunk after dinner when he sold Jacob and Margaret, he was higher than the moon by the time he returned from the hunt. Laura figured he was well asleep now up in his room, where he would more than likely stay, well into morning.

She moved with bitter determination. For a good while now she had been wondering just how long she could hold on to cooking and not doctoring up the food with some extra tidbit of her own. "An eye for an eye," kept coming into her mind: Marse Stone and Missus Rosalan for Ben and Jimmy and all of the others over the years. One day she figured that the stew pot which she managed so well would fix the Stone's into the very ground. One day, if she didn't die first.

Tom Wilson, the overseer, was bedded down, too, drunker than Marse Stone. Laura had her ways of finding and sending out information. Most of the guards were over at Jonah's shack getting their share of corn liquor and swapping tales. The dogs were chained to their kennels and too well fed on Jimmy to howl. Nobody was out but Laura near the big house and Marse Bowan down the cabins with Jacob, and maybe old man death was still out wandering.

Laura reached the window. The cricket sounded beside her foot, but she put what she was thinking out of her mind. Killing anything went the wrong way with her, but killing a cricket was bad luck, and killing a black cricket was double bad.

"Peta—Peta." Her voice was quiet. She tapped her fingernails against the glass.

Not a light in the sky, neither star nor moon and lots of clouds to make the night obscure. A good strong breeze was puffing down from the north. Good signs; muddy gray-black sky and a northern wind.

"Peta—Peta, man. Don't make no noise," Laura's fingers tapped out a waiting rhythm as she thought how glad she was that poor Jimmy had been alone in this world. It was sad for him to grow up with no mother or father to love him, and sadder still that he hadn't found himself a woman to call his at night, but it was good to have no mother or sweetheart to grieve for him now that he was gone; nor a father or brother to die trying to avenge him. Folks other than kinfolks had been crying enough. Three of his friends, Joe, Charlie and William, with a couple of guards walking behind them, had gotten permission to find what was left of Jimmy's body down in the woods. The dogs had done their work on Jimmy after the shooting. She just prayed that Jimmy was dead when they reached him.

She could hear Peter moving in his room. Laura moved toward the celler door as Peter unbolted it.

She slipped inside and headed straight for Peter's room. They spoke to each other cautiously in the darkness, each one sounding short of breath from the tension of their conspiracy.

"Peta, Marse Bowan done bought Jacob and Margaret from Marse Stone. Marse Bowan say he want Margaret tonight so's Missus won't stop him from taking her north. I come for the girl."

Peter shook his head. His voice was harsh. "White man sho know his stuff. He tell you he buy two people, flesh and soul, two people you knows, and he tell you to go bring one of 'em, a child of a girl, outta the big house in the middle of the night. How you know he ain't stealin' 'em? How you know he ain't trickin' you so Marse can shoot you dead for fun? How you dare help a white man buy a black slave? Laura, you musta loss your mind."

Laura bristled and walked toward Peter. She couldn't see him or anything else in the dark. The room was pitch, but his voice was enough to aim at.

"First place, Sue Anne tol' me after dinner she heard Marse Stone and Marse Bowan talking tonight in the study. She heard Margaret's name at dinner so she went to the China cabinent near the grate in the wall next to the study and listen whilst she put the china away. Marse Stone done sold Maraget and Jacob for a whul lota money. Sue Anne says Marse were drunk as she ever seed him. Say he took the money and tol' Marse Bowan to git outta his house.

"Secund place, Marse Bowan save Jacob from them guards today. He brung me supplies—food and cloth over a week ago to help me out. I seen the look on his face when he seed Tom Wilson beat Helen three day ago for trying to run away. Tom beat that child so hard folks could hear her crying and shoutin' way out in the fields. Marse Bowan come outta the house a-flyin' 'cause Helen was screaming so hard. He seed what Tom was doin and he looked like he'd been shot." Laura smiled. He whupped Tom Wilson like he was a nigger man." Laura chuckled to herself.

"An one mo'e thing. Jacob headed to die if he stay here. He headed to die a white man's gift a death. Anything better than this place. Margaret ain't got no hope. Marse Stone gonna take her one night. She gone be the next Cook Laura if she stay. Raped every nite that she's young. We gots to gamble. Then too, Jacob is strong, and he hate all the white mens already. If Marse Bowan don't mind hisself, Jacob put a knife in him."

Peter sucked absently at his teeth and reached for the door knob. Whether he helped Laura or not, she would get what she came for, even if she had to knock Margaret's door down. Missy Rosalan thought she had the only key to Margaret's room. She put the girl into her small room at night and let her out every morning so her husband couldn't get to her, but Peter had a key. He and the smithy and Laura had collaborated on a key long ago, and at least one night a week, Laura came sneaking in the dark. She would get the key from Peter and the girl would visit with some of her friends down in the quarters. Margaret had never been able to say a word in gratitude to Laura, and Laura couldn't read a thing the girl wrote down on paper, but they understood each other. Peter figured the girl would have died by now if Laura hadn't found a way to regularly free her from that room.

Without another word Peter opened the door and guided Laura into the hall. His hand pressed against her palm leaving the cold metal key in her hand.

Margaret Collins passed through the cellar door of the big house, her right hand still warm with the goodbye touch of Peter's hand. The butler closed the door behind her, his "Lord God bless you" soft on her ear. Laura was walking just ahead of Margaret, a small sack under her arm. She had told Margaret about Marse Bowan's promise of freedom, and the girl was full of fear. Mixed with the fear was a small and cautious trace of hope that her dream of leaving slavery might be approaching reality.

Every twig she stepped on made her quake inside, down around her stomach and up near her heart. She could trust Cook Laura. She had no doubts about Cook Laura, but Lord, what about Marse Davis Bowan? She had heard some of his words while she was serving dinner, and they hadn't sounded kind. What could he want of her that was anything but bad? At least she hadn't been physically molested under Rosalan Stone's protection. She had never been more than a slave and servant. Her freedom had never been hers, but she had been relatively safe from actual harm and physical abuse. She had learned the things which only white women learned; reading, writing, fine needle work and piano playing. She figured that her good fortune, in this sense, was paid for by the color of her skin. Missy Rosalan had even told her once that she was not like the others. The whole class system had been explained over the years. Light skinned niggers, the yellows up to creme, were better than the brown ones, and the brown ones were farther up from satan than the black ones. Nobody darker than medium brown was even allowed to set foot in the house, except for Cook Laura and Peter, and he had been the child of an old cook that Marse Stone's mother had doted on. To be creme, however, with

blond hair and blue eyes, put a nigger in a special
boat. Next to the family and the landed neighbors,
friends and guests and poor white trash, no one was
higher on the scale. And Margaret should be proud.

That's just how Missy Rosalan had put it that day.
Margaret Collins should be proud. Margaret was
proud, but it had nothing to do with Rosalan Stone or
with her own coloring.

Margaret clutched Laura's bony hand as they moved
out across the yard. Laura never missed a stride. She
walked past the hedgerow and through the back fence
toward the barn. She had preached and prayed to
Margaret to get her to come and even now the girl was
reluctant. Laura began talking in a whisper.

"Things has they time, child. We comes into dis world
not knowing much of anything, and we tries to make
the best we can. You is too young to be scart to do
something new. That kinda talk is fur old folks set on
dying. You got to take the chances the Lawd give you
and go like you been blessed by Jesus hisself.'' An owl,
perched low and hidden in a nearby tree, sent a series
of hoots adrift over the yard. Margaret felt a chill pass
over her. She took a deep breath and kept up with the
old woman marching by her side.

"Marse Bowan may a fooled me. He may be like 'em
all. I kin only go by how he make me feel. He ain't no
ord'nary mean white man. He look to me like he got a
peck a coloured in him somewheres.'' Laura chuckled
to herself. "He a sight better'n Marse Stone.

Laura slowed her gait and then stopped. Jacob and
Bowan were rigging a wagon a few hundred feet away.
The horses were already hitched and standing in their
traces.

"If I is wrong about Marse Bowan, I has a plan to fix
him for his lying.'' Laura turned Margaret's hand over
and across the palm she laid a skinning knife. The
blade was well honed and curved at the tip to a sharp

point. Margaret could just see the bare shadow of the blade, long and thin and sharp against her hand. "If you leave here and that white man treat you wrong any kind a way, take this here knife and kill him. Don't let him git away with treatin' you wrong. I'se gonna give Jacob one, too. Now Bowan say he's agin slavery, and all he come south for was to buy two or three slaves and give'em safe pasage north—and he say he be giving you a purse a money to start. Well, if he's lying you get away and pretend you white if you has to."

There were so many words milling in Margaret's head, so many things she wanted to say. She opened her mouth and tried to speak. Laura placed her hand over the girl's mouth. It pained her to hear the choked and unintelligible mumblings the girl made. "No chil', you don't have to try to say nothing."

Margaret turned away. She knew she could never use the knife. The thought of it made her feel weak. It was no good. She would be better off if she stayed. Laura caught Margaret's arm and turned her around.

"Now you listens to me, Margaret, and you listens good to me. You kain't get weak on me now. How you think we done made this life last so long? How you think my mother and her mother stayed alive long enough for me to come in this world? You ain't never done a thing in your days but sit in that house. You past seventeen this summer, and you been in a fancy jail all that time. But you seen all the womens in the field. You heard the whip singing. You heard the crying and moaning from the cabins. You tasted the hominy and grease we has to eat. You watched me steal everything I kin get my hands on to feed them chilluns out back there. You knows what's waiting for you from Marse Stone, and for your chilluns when they is born. Child, you is young and you is a slave down here. They's one chance you got, and I'll wack you on the head and carry you myself before I see you turn around now." Laura pulled the girl to her and hugged her. The old woman was much shorter than Margaret, and her frame was slight, but she gripped the girl more with her heart than with her arms.

"Don't you fret child. The Lawd and Jacob gonna see you th'ough. You trust in Jacob. He's a strong man. Now hide dat knife in your dress and hold your head up high. You'se got a long trip to go, and you'll be wanting the sun way behind you by the time you git on the main road. When Missy Rosalan find out you sold she gone try to get you back."

Jacob and Bowan were waiting on the wagon. Margaret followed Laura, her steps hesitant but determined. She looked back over her shoulder at the huge white framed house which loomed ghostlike through the darkness. She could hear the wind rattling the window curtains, and the rasp of regular snoring was coming from the east room; Marse Stone's room. She thought of how surprised Missy Rosalan would be when she unlocked the celler door and found the room empty.

A kind of joy, a feeling of triumph like she had never known, rushed through her. She remembered the years of playing the quaint human toy to Missy Rosalan's guests; a reading, writing mute white nigger slave girl, and a shiver of joy shot through her. No more. No more to stand in the middle of the drawing room floor, her hair falling in curls about her shoulders and her body clothed in a frilly dress, all chosen especially to amuse. "Her intelligence must come from her father," one of them would say and they would all laugh.

"No one can tell me that her affliction didn't come from her nigger mother and the sin she was born in."

"My word, ladies, don't talk so in front of the girl. She can hear, you know. I won't have her insulted. She is really a dear child, though I must admit, when John

first brought her home I couldn't get used to the fact
that she never cried aloud. It was some time before we
learned from Doctor Rogers that she couldn't talk. He
said he didn't know what the trouble was, but he knew
she could hear. I had to teach her to read so I could
communicate with her."

"Well, I guess that makes her a freak of nature all the
way around. Her mother was a black nigger and she's
as white of skin as I am. Her throat looks normal and
she can't talk. Lord have mercy, I know Clara Harris
must turn green everytime somebody mentions your
name, Rosalan. If my husband had fathered such a
child, why, my word, Clara must look at him and hate
him every minute."

"Yes, I imagine she does." Rosalan laughed heartily
and had to wipe tears away from her eyes.

"Well, dear, it is interesting that she has learned to
read words so accurately. And her handwriting is
rather pretty, considering. You must bring her to tea
next Sunday. I'm having guests from Atlanta. They'll
be amused off their feet to see this child."

And on and on for as far back as Margaret could
remember. It was good to reach out in the darkness
toward Laura and to share her joy at the promise of
freedom. It was good to sit upon a wagon bed with
horses pulling and another world waiting. It was good
to think about the sunrise, and the key turning old
and cranky in the lock, and the door opening a hole of
light into the dank little room, where Rosalan Stone,
God bless her cruel kindness, would stand alone and
bewildered at the sight of no Margaret to greet her.

Part II

On the bed of her 25th year, she conceived. Within
three months time, the child was aborted. Again, on
another night, and on the same Virginia bed, her
second child was conceived. This child died before it

was old enough to be born. Twice her husband took her and she joined with her part in the making of an offspring. It was not good enough that the conceptions left her childless. If she could not have a voice in her own life, if everything else was empty and insane, she determined that she would bring a living soul into the world who might, in crying its first cry, express all of the soundless anguish of her long silence.

Her doctor thought it unwise for her to conceive again, and her husband reluctantly agreed. But she was determined, and so on the evening of January 16, 1869, she lay in labor upon that same death visited bed, eight months pregnant and afraid.

The delivery could have been so lovely a series of moments, despite the pain. She had waited a long time, and had come close to death both in miscarrying and in her dreams. In her childhood days of slavery and serving in the Georgia big house, she had often dared dream of marriage and bearing children. As surely as she hoped for freedom, she had hoped to see a child of hers running with the sweetness of its own life. It could have been, when this labor began, the beginning of her own birth. It could have been had she not married the man who was her husband and lived with him throughout their marriage. All possibility of joy died when he chose to marry her, and for ten years, with two children dead before she knew their faces and small killing torments etched from month to year in her memory, she would not admit how impossible her dream had always been. She would not face it until she heard on the swelling shouts of her husband's angry voice, several hours before this bout of labor pains began, to what end and in what form her dreams would die.........Like God. Like God he stood over their unconsecrated wedding bed and preached out her sentence. "You are my wife. You are free to be what you are told to be, to do what you are told to do. Your days, your nights, your youth, your beauty are mine. You *will* be my wife, to punish me for killing Jacob, to punish you for rejecting me for him. You will reign as mistress of my household, serve me as wife and mother of my children and work among my black so-called freedmen for all your mortal life. It is no good in playing the fool. I am no emancipator of men or virtue. I tried and I failed, and if my minute victory over you has taught me nothing else, it has taught me that I must keep you, to remind me of my foul mistakes and of your murderous guilt." So now, in labor, with little or no awareness of where she was, she lay in spasmodic pain, crying wretched tears and praying to her God that she and her unborn child might die.

"It's almost time, Margaret," Dr. Grandby said as he mopped sweat from her face. "You must bear down when the time comes."

Bear down, she thought, I will not bear anything. I will not. My child must die inside of me. She smiled, knowing Dr. Granby could not hear or understand her shouted thoughts. He took her smile as encouragement, patted her hand gratefully and returned to the foot of the bed where he stood waiting for her child. He knew that her marriage had been unhappy and that he liked her and was in great sympathy.

There was very little light in the room. Dr. Granby had it all with him, down where her legs were propped apart and he was waiting to do his work. There was someone else, a young black woman, brown as Cook Laura had been brown when Margaret left her. Margaret shook her head sadly and wondered if Laura was still alive. She could still feel the comforting presence of the old woman. "Oh, Laura, how awful life has been to me, except for you and Jacob."

The room, its light, the doctor, the brown woman were a splintered vision as though she was looking through some well picked block of once solid ice. They moved and spoke outwardly calm though they were anxious and weary with waiting and worrying. Others came, and became three brown women, one very dark, who all held her thrashing body firmly against the bed. Margaret could hear herself screaming, though they heard only the mumblings and jumbled screams of a woman dumb since birth.

"Do you know who I am? Do you? You three watching me? I am Mrs. Margaret Collins Bowan, mistress of this house, surrounded by the slavery of this harassed company, and my child must only be *his* child. Not mine. Do you know? Do you understand? How could you know? Why won't you hear me?" The words were clanging like a broken bell inside of her skull. The empty clanging would surely drive her mad.

"You can't talk? Is that it? Margaret, is that why you haven't spoken a word to Jacob or me since we left Stone's place? Is it?" Davis Bowan held her by her shoulders so she couldn't turn away. He had offered to help her collect wood for the campfire and inevitably, he had begun to talk, to ask her opinion of leaving slavery. She could not answer. Jacob came up behind them.

"That's it, Marse Bowan," he said. "She kain't speak a word. She were born that way."

"Are you going to take me back, now?" She wanted to ask. "We're just two days travel from Rosalan Stone. Are you going to take the dumb soul of me back?" Margaret watched Bowan anxiously. Bowan dropped his hands and sat down on a stump. "Forgive me for blurting it out like that, but I knew something was wrong, and I didn't want to believe you were so frightened of me that you wouldn't say a single word."

Margaret felt the tears of her shame trickling down her face. She looked at Bowan, still seated and stunned. Jacob seemed unconcerned with Bowan. His steady gaze held her eyes, softly. She wanted most to

talk with Jacob. Of all the people in the world, she
wanted a voice for him. He was the only comfort she
could count on. But Jacob couldn't read her writing.
She couldn't tell him what she thought of him or the
world. Bowan could read, but she was ashamed of her
soundless throat before him. He made her flaws seem
so obvious. At this moment she needed Bowan's
acceptance as well as Jacob's. He and Jacob were the
only people she knew, now. Without their understanding and help she was alone and a cripple. She was
ashamed, and even more, she was afraid that like
some horse or cow born deformed, Bowan would reject
her and return her to Rosalan's lock and key. She ran
away from them both, past the first few trees and
toward the deeper woods. Bowan soon caught her and
once again turned her to face him. "Please, forgive me
for being so clumsy. I didn't know. It never crossed
my mind until you couldn't answer my questions and
even then I didn't want to believe it. I found out like a
fool." Bowan lead her back to their camp. She was too
upset to protest.

Jacob stood away when they returned and felt a rage
coming over him. Bowan had ordered him to remain
with the horses and wagon, and after a lifetime of taking orders he responded out of an old reflex. He swore
to himself that this would never happen again. In his
mind, although he had not yet said a word of it to
Margaret, he claimed her as his own. They were a
pair, two almost free slaves, a man and a woman
almost free. Bowan had no right to touch her in any
way.

During the next weeks, Bowan took her for walks and
spoke to her protectively of what the world of being
free was like. He provided her with paper, ink and pen
and asked questions so she could answer. She
wouldn't write a word without prodding. Days went by
and he saw her laughing and gay for the first time.
Their travels brought them to Atlanta. The city was a

revelation to her. They were there for two days, and during the first few hours she did not notice that Jacob walked behind them. Bowan brought her lovely dresses and presented her on the streets and in the shops as a lady, a beautiful lady whose hair was golden, whose eyes were blue, whose complexion was fair. She looked into a mirror while a white shopkeeper placed a ribboned bonnet upon her head. The face, the body, the woman looking back at her was not a nigger, but a free born white woman, and her escort had the money and the complexion to make her so if she wanted. She began thinking herself a white lady and might have clung to the illusion had she not turned in the midst of her elation and seen Jacob, his eyes blazing at her with dismay and anger. He was standing outside of the shop window with his arms full of brown paper-wrapped packages. He did not soften his look as she walked past him. Bowan motioned them out into the street, and Jacob answered, with an exaggerated "Yas, suh." The illusion burst. Her shame cast a heaviness over her. It was Bowan, not Jacob, who was the outcast in this company. She vowed never to forget again.

One day in the middle of September, somewhere in northern South Carolina, when the sun was hidden in a gray blare behind a sky of fall clouds, Jacob took Margaret by the hand and led her away from the noon cooking fire. It was their custom to rest an hour after each meal. Since Davis had learned about her speechlessness and they had become friends, Margaret had begun to relax. Although he offered her unaccustomed genteel male company with his fine manners and his outgoing spirit, she preferred Jacob, and loved to walk with him when the day's travel was momentarily put aside. She loved his long stride and the color of his face and hands, dark and strong, as he laughed and gestured with his words. She loved the way he found special things to show her; an oddly shaped tree or a lilly pad blossoming all alone on a shallow lake.

He had taken Laura's words to heart, from that first night. He never allowed her to be lonely or troubled without telling her he was with her, and he joked black folk's jokes and reminisced over the good times Laura and Ben and all of the black folk she missed so when she closed her eyes. He recalled things about her childhood which Laura had told him, and which Margaret had forgotten. He brought back the sweet familiar things of living among the signaling songs: "Brother, Where Shall I Send Thee?", "Swing Low", "Steal Away." He was her home.

He had learned to read her moods by the set of her mouth and the look in her eyes, and often told her so. Every night for weeks now he sat beside her after supper and practiced writing. He was an eager student. How could she answer him or tell him what her eyes only hinted at if he couldn't read her writing? How could he know directly why she came to a sudden smile or stared off into the distance like some ghost had just passed her by? He said he wanted to know, and he would learn. With Bowan's help and her inspiration, he was well on his way.

"I wants to show you something. I ain't seen one since I was a boy," he said as he lead her along a footpath toward a clearing. She walked gayly, feeling a pleasure and a freedom she had never known. The woods was made of pine, the trees tall and fine in their greenery. The forest floor was deep with needle padding, and whispered as their feet pressed them to the ground. Ahead of them lay a fast running river, and along its narrow bend, a small abandoned mill house. The paddles in the huge wheel were still and broken.

"I seen me one a them wheels when I was a boy," Jacob said. "Marse Harris took me on a trip one time to git some wheat ground. I wasn't much taller than a scrubby pine, so all that day, I sat doing nothing but watching the water move the wheel. It sure was something." Jacob fondly squeezed Margaret's hand as he led her across a narrow foot bridge and into the mill house.

The mill house was barren except for several grain bags, old and rotted into holes. The floor was strewn with empty wheat hulls, mingled with flour and dust. Cob webs hung in great patches from every rafter, and a couple of birds, startled by the human intrusion, fluttered out into the sky through a jagged hole in the roof.

"Some man put his back into this place once. I guess the stream let him and his water wheel down. I wonders who used to stand over there and guide the big millstone whilst it crushed the grain?" Margaret shook her head and raised her hands as if to say, who knows, and Jacob laughed and said, "Come on over here. There's one more thing." He lead her to the far side of the building where some of the boards in the wall had rotted away. They looked out onto a gentle slope which wound down through a sparse growth of long needle pine to the river, bent and rocky on the other side.

"This here is a fine place. Look at that land, and over there, the way the river curls around. I kin see me a little house at the top of the rise, and grazing land near the water for cows and a horse or two." Margaret was standing close beside him, and he hugged her as he talked. She leaned her head against his chest and listened as he dreamed.

"I planned it different in my head. I told myse'f I was gonna court you slow like until this trip was over, and then after I got myself a little piece of land I'd speak my mind. But I knows better than to wait, now. I knows better." Jacob paused. He seemed nervous and stared into the distance as though he expected to draw courage from it. "Come on, the grass is so pretty. Maybe if we sets down I can talk better."

Margaret climbed over the vacant top of the millhouse foundation and ran a good ways down the slope where

the grass was deep and green. Jacob caught up with
her and started to sit down. He thought better of it,
bowed from the waist and held out his hand to assist
Margaret. "Ma*dam*, would you mind sitting so I can
do the same?" Margaret curtsied and sat down in a
flourish. They both laughed and took each other in
with appreciation.

Margaret was radiant. Her dress was a pale yellow and
all around her the world was green and red and
brown. "My, my, if you ain't a pretty sight sitting in
the middle of my pasture." He laughed again, and as
their eyes met and the looking lengthened into a long
spell of time, the mischief and the lighthearted grins
faded into serious looks of appraisal and appreciation.

"I never knew me many words, Margaret. There
wasn't much time for pretty talk, the way things was. I
wish I could find me some pretty words, to help me
say what's on my mind. I first knew what I wanted
to say on that night we left Laura. The way you cried
with your head resting against my arm, and the way
you held onto me all the days and nights after that,
like you was scared to death to be alone. Something in
me said 'hold on to her and promise her things is
gonna be good from now on.' I wanted to take you in
my arms that first night and just hold you until you
stopped crying so bad." He laughed. "I did manage to
git my arm around your shoulder, after awhile, but I
was nervous. And then I seen Davis sweet talking you
and buying you with clothes and pretty words and a
chance for you to play act at being white. I got scared
because I knowed I could never give to you what he
do, and the Lawd knows I kain't make you no white
woman. I got scared and angry and I prayed your
head wouldn't turn."

A flock of swallows flew over head, and Jacob pointed
them out as they frolicked over the millhouse and
disappeared among the pine trees. "That's how I
wants us to be. Free to go and to fly. One day I'm
gonna have me a farm. My own piece a land. And one

day I'm gonna have my own children, pretty free
children that no white man kin take away. I'll be
needing a good wife . . . ." He felt his courage
leaving him. "And if . . . if you . . . ."

Margaret sat up on her knees, a look of happiness on
her face. Her hand moved down along his cheek until
her fingers came to rest against his lips. She took his
hand into hers and pressed his fingers gently to her
mouth, kissing them.

"Oh, Lord, if you could only say what I wants to hear
you say," Jacob said as he leaned closer until he could
feel her lips touch his own hand. She moved his hand
away and his mouth covered hers with a long deep
kiss. The taste of all of his desire throbbed and grew
as he took her into his arms and pressed the soft
shape of her bosom against him. He thought the world
was spinning crazy as she relaxed to the pressure of
his body and kissed him while the first tears he had
ever seen her shed for joy trickled down her face and
mingled with the sweet of her mouth. He felt tears
coming to his own eyes and let them flow as he eased
beside her on the grass and held her to him.

"Oh, Margrit Collins, I've got to find me a good last
name. I've got to find me a name so's I kin give it
away again."

By that old pond, oily green with powder blue clouds
folding into the sky and looping past on a sudden
wind; by that old pond where they rested, four days
journey from the Chesapeake, and the Eastern Shore
of Virginia, beyond; Rosalan Stone's guardianship a
hazy, wintry childhood thing, and her feet hanging off

the edge of a rickety dock into the water, Margaret sat calm and reflecting the day, silent and peaceful.

She thought of how it must be to exist and not to be a person. To be a tree or a lake or a granite wall. They must be full of thoughts as people are, as I am, she whispered inside of her head. That tall pine, that cottonwood with its pods turned dry, brown and empty of seed. Surely they are thinking and hurting like me because they cannot tell it to a soul.

Davis walked around the edge of the pond. The sleeves of his ruffled shirt were rolled to the elbows, and sweat had left his pants damp at the knees. He carried a small bottle of ink, a pen and some paper in his hands. He had done almost as much physical labor as Jacob since the trip began. This surprised Margaret. It was a strange thing to see a white man of wealth involved in the common labor of driving a loaded wagon across stretches of wilderness and bending his back under a hot sun when fallen trees blocked the way. It was even more strange to hear Jacob calling him Davis. Jacob had not found the transition difficult from all she could tell. He made each day count in his journey away from slavery. Bowan had been very kind and helpful most of the way. He seemed slightly annoyed at giving Jacob reading lessons, but he was tired by the end of a long day. All this time he hadn't said a word about his fight with Jacob in the cotton field on the first day they had met. It was almost as if it hadn't happened. Sometimes he lost patience with Jacob and swore under his breath, but he knew better than to push him too far. He was almost careful of what he said. Most careful.

"Well, my lady," Davis said as he sat beside her, "Don't you look comfortable luxuriating in the sun." Margaret smiled and pointed toward the pond. She pointed at the sun and the large gathering of ducks paddling along the far shore.

"Yes, they are lovely, aren't they," Davis said. "You look happy; happier than I've seen you, like your soul is full of well being. I've brought you pen and paper. Now you can talk to me in your fashion." He placed them beside her and began removing his shoes and socks.

"We're almost home, you know," he said as he stuck his feet into the warm water. "Ah, that feels good. A few days more and we'll board a ship for the Bay crossing, and once across, within three hours we'll be pulling up at my door. What do you think of that?"

Margaret wrote, "I am excited and relieved, and I am uncertain. I can't help wondering what will become of Jacob and me."

He read her words and laid back against the dock. "I hope life for both of you will be good. I plan to give Jacob a stake. I think he will be happier in some state further north of Virginia. A freedman in Virginia has a difficult way to go." Bowan let his head fall to the side. He rose on his elbow and traced the form of Margaret's hand with his fingers.

"Your hands are lovely, Margaret. They're soft and slender. As for the rest of you, there are no words." Bowan laughed softly to himself. "There are no words good enough. I have plans for you, my girl, if you will agree. But, before I tell you about them, let me tell you something more about myself."

Margaret pulled her feet out of the water and wrapped them in a towel. She glanced over her shoulder toward Jacob. He was sitting by the wagon, repairing some harness that had come undone. He was good at leather work. She thought of that day by the mill and the lovely glow which had come over her since. Jacob was a beautiful man, broadly muscled and gentle with his words. She missed his company though he was close at hand. When they reached the town of Eastville where Bowan lived, she and Jacob would spend a few days getting their bearings, and then the two of them would leave together. Jacob hoped to find work in Pennsylvania until he could earn enough to buy a piece of land. He wasn't counting on a stake from Bowan, but had said that if one was offered he would take it as a small payment against all of the years of slave labor taken from him. He expected things to be hard at first, but it was a far cry better than slavery. They would find a way, and they would make it.

Once out of the southern states they would be married. She wondered if she could stand the wait until they found a country preacher, some old black man with graying hair and the look of God's eternal inspiration on his face as he married them to each other for all their lives.

"Margaret, you're not being attentive," Bowan said, interrupting her thoughts. "Come now, I have a story to tell you. It's very important to me that you listen." She turned her full attention to him, putting her shoes and stockings aside.

"That's better," he said. "Look me full in the face while I tell you a brief history. I was born in London, England, and lived there until I was ten or so, when my only living parent, my father, died and left me alone. He was a rich man, my father, and very kind to me. He inherited a fortune when his father died leaving him the family shipping industry. The company was begun by my great grandfather, who joined in partnership with a wealthy gentleman. Great grandfather was poor and young and as crafty as a weasel, I'm told. Well, this deal turned out to be a lucrative venture. They began with two ships which made lovely scenic voyages to the coast of West Africa. No doubt your grandmother or maybe her mother traveled to America in the dank hold of one of them. Transporting slaves to the New World filled great granddad's pockets with gold. He bought more ships, dissolved his partnership and passed the loot on for generations.''

Margaret looked over the pond, remembering the stories she had heard about slave ships. She had always wondered how anyone had survived. Her mood was changing. A sickening anger was growing in her chest. Bowan spoke so lightly of his ugly heritage. He seemed unaware of the meaning and impact of his own words, and this amazed her. Or did he think that she was a fool?

"I don't know which way my life would have turned if my cousin in America hadn't taken me on. It was arranged that I live with him in New York. I enjoyed his gracious hospitality until I came of age and then I set out on my own. I went into busines, real estate, merchant ships, shopkeeping and the fur trade. I invested thousands and felt no real joy doing anything.

"Finally I became involved with a group of abolitionists. I won't go into that, but the important thing is that I found something to commit myself to. I contributed large sums to the movement and debated the issue of slavery with my friends. I thought I knew what I was doing and saying. But I didn't really. Slavery was still just a word to me. I felt no responsibility. So what if my money was made at the cost of other men's freedom. My foreparents, another generation, had done that. I was not to blame, and I was doing something about the problem. But then, one day, shortly after I purchased my land in Virginia, I attended a slave auction in Eastville. I saw men women and children made to strip naked before the gawking eyes of white gentlefolk. I saw the despair and the wretchedness wrapped like an ugly plague infested sheet about their lives. I suddenly knew it was my duty to accomplish something more than I already had; to find a way to end the misery and the hypocracy." Bowan spit the words harshly from his mouth. Margaret nodded her head, relieved to know that he held such strong anti-slavery convictions. Her earlier judgment of him must be wrong.

"Buying slaves became an obsession with me. I was determined to personally buy as many slaves as I could, and then to set them free with enough money to get them further north. I did most of my work in Virginia and Maryland. I had discovered a special purpose for living. I had found a cause to fully give myself to . I, Davis Bowan, made rich from the slave trade, would free the black multitudes. Not with prayers and preachings and begging, but with hard cash!" Bowan stopped talking to catch his breath. He sat forward and took a leaky handful of water from the pond, dashing his face with it.

Margaret wrote, "Then you are a man of great conviction. You have helped to set slaves free. To correct a great wrong."

"Yes, in a way, but it wasn't enough. I was searching for something when I met you. Something really fine to do, and in the instant of seeing you, I suddenly knew the answer. I suddenly knew the ultimate act to set myself right with my own conscience."

Margaret was puzzled. She could not quite understand what Davis meant, and what meeting her had to do with it. Something about his tone was possessive and almost ominous.

"I've watched you intently since this trip got underway," he said, shielding his eyes from the sun as it slipped from behind a mass of clouds. "You're a beautiful woman. You're still very young, but you're already a woman. How old are you, Margaret?"

She wrote, "Laura thinks I'm seventeen, and I thought so too until I asked Mrs. Stone one day. She said I was born in the early summer of 1838, so that would make me twenty."

"Twenty, a marvelous age to be. You know, you looked at home when we shopped in Atlanta. There's a definite style about you, a grace in your walk and in the tilt of your bonnet." Bowan leaned closer to her.

"You are very kind," she wrote. "Jacob thinks I look best in yellow. I think so too. He likes the yellow dress and bonnet better than the blue."

"Yes." Bowan said, frowning. "I've noticed your frequent walks with Jacob. It disturbs me, Margaret. Jacob is, well, he's not your style, not refined enough, if you know what I mean. He can't even speak a decent sentence. I have better things in mind for you. Lovely clothes, finer than these, and a world of riches, gay company, a life the complete reversal of any you've known or could possibly dream of."

A frown began at the apex of Margaret's eyebrows. The corners of her mouth moved downward as she turned from Bowan and reached for her shoes. She felt a trace of her old fear coming through the air to greet her like an omen of evil. Bowan took her hand and she eased it away. She didn't want to offend him, but was beginning to understand that beneath his gentility, he was offensive. She sensed that he was a powerful man to cross.

"What are you thinking," Bowan asked, an urgency working its way into his voice. "Tell me. Write it down."

Margaret picked up the pen. She wanted the conversation to end now. She didn't want to hear any more of Davis Bowan's plans. She wrote, "I love Jacob, Mr Bowan. He has asked me to marry him, and I plan to become his wife as soon as possible."

Bowan took the paper, and slowly, a look of disbelief clouded his face.

"You must be joking. You can't marry that clod. You mean to tell me that you would choose him over me, over all I can give you?" His face was red and his mouth was angry. "You can't do this. My plans. Our marriage is the answer, don't you see? Jacob is a fiend, a killer. He attacked me in Stone's field for no reason at all, and if I hadn't been forgiving and benevolent, Stone would have whipped him to death. His violent nature would crush you inside of a year."

Margaret felt a jolt of fright and shock as Bowan gripped her wrist and held her as she tried to stand. She couldn't believe he had changed so much in so short a time. He looked like some other man; John Stone or Robert Lawrence or even Tom Wilson with his bitter lashing tongue. The terror of twenty years of white treachery overcame her mind and judgement. Margaret jerked her hand away, got to her feet and ran down the swaying dock toward Jacob. Jacob looked up from his work and jumped to his feet as she passed him and ducked around the back of the wagon. She was pale and obviously frightened of Bowan.

"He's too black for you, girl." Bowan shouted as he came on the run. "Don't you see. He's not fit to touch you." Bowan rushed around the wagon and jerked her around roughly by her arm. "Don't run from me. You haven't listened to a word I've said all afternoon. Didn't you learn anything from Rosalan Stone?" Margaret beat frantically at his hand holding her wrist. Bowan wrestled around until he grasped her free hand. He increased his grip on her wrists until he was obviously hurting her. She struggled for another second and then froze with the awful realization of what she had done to Jacob. She *was* a fool. She had surely provoked Jacob and as she looked into his face she knew it was too late.

"Let her go," Jacob shouted angrily. His voice, quite unexpected, broke sharply into Bowan's hearing.

"You heard me, Davis, let her go." Jacob stepped closer, brandishing the leather cutting knife.

"Stay out of this, Jacob. This is none of your affair." Margaret's eyes were fixed on the knife and the almost crazy look of anger on Jacob's face. Jacob took a step closer. "I ain't a slave no more *Marse* Bowan. Now, you take your hands off a her, and do it now."

"Jacob, get the hell . ." Jacob struck Bowan across the mouth and sent him sprawling to the ground. He pushed Margaret gently away from them toward the wagon and then turned to Bowan. Davis was badly shaken as he stood and wiped at the blood on his mouth. "You've gone too far this time, Jacob. I took your violence in Georgia because I thought I understood, but I won't take it anymore."

Jacob took a step closer. "Understand. You don't know nothin' but what you thinks you know, and your head's too thick to learn."

"Put the knife back where you found it, man. I'm warning you. I still own you, you know."

"White man, you don't own a hair on my head." Jacob shouted. He jumped at Bowan with the knife and went into a semi-crouch. Bowan stumbled backwards and almost lost his footing. He took quick glances around. There was nothing behind him but the pond, and he couldn't swim a stroke. His only chance was to reach the wagon.

"Ever since I been born, white mens been doing and saying what they please to coloured women, and ain't nobody ever done nothing about it. Well, this here is one black man that's gonna do plenty, and there ain't nobody to whup me this time. I take my freedom. You hear. I take my freedom and my woman. You don't give me nothing."

"I was foolishly angry, Jacob," Bowan said as he moved step by step in a semi-circle toward the wagon. "I didn't mean it the way it sounded." He raised his hands in front of himself and pushed through the air as though there was some object touching him that he was defending his life against. "You'd be crazy to harm me. People, white people are all over this area. They'll hang you if you even try to harm me. I'll see you hanged.''

Margaret found her senses and rushed to stop Jacob. She grabbed at his arm and tried to push herself between the knife and Bowan.

"Git away, Margaret," Jacob's voice trembled with rage. "I'm gonna fight for my own this time. Move away." He rolled the knife around in his hand as he stepped closer to Bowan. Margaret screamed as best she could. She pounded Jacob's wrist and struggled for the knife. He *couldn't* kill Bowan. He would surely die if he did that.

Bowan broke into a run and reached the wagon seat before Jacob could get himself free of Margaret. He reached into a carpet bag and pulled frantically through the contents, throwing clothes and other personal items, and glancing over his shoulder as his hand searched around in the bag and finally closed on what he was looking for. He started to turn as Jacob came at a run across the small patch of ground between them. Jacob reached for Bowan's shoulder and thrust the knife forward as Bowan swung around. The knife fell short and stopped in mid-air as Bowan fired a shot point blank into Jacob's chest. The gunfire echoed across the pond into the massive stand of spruce trees standing like sentinels to the open land beyond. Ducks squawked in fright and rose in a confused and noisey cloud above the water. One of the horses, tied to a tree, reared and broke its halter rope. The beat of hooves pounded for a long while down the hard packed road. Margaret stood numb and frozen as she saw a small jagged hole of torn cloth and blood appear in the middle of Jacob's back. His shoulders rounded down and drew inward like they were being pulled together by some terrible crushing hand. He made a gurgling, painful sound and slumped to the ground. She heard his last breath in a moan as it passed out of him into the open air.

For ten years Bowan had lived up to his promise, and for ten years she had merely lived, surrounded by the horror of that day when she helped to kill the only loveliness she had ever known. She had lived to be the mute and barely seen mistress over slaves who looked at her, cursed her and swore to God against her white skin. She had lived to see a war rage and tear the ground from under a slavery that still wouldn't die while the shock of losing Jacob crept more deeply day by day into her consciousness, disabling her will. There were times when she lost track of days on end. And just before the labor pains had begun to separate her bones, she dared to ask him if she could tell their child that he or she was partially black, a child of slavery, whose great grandmother and grandmother died bearing the rubbing marks of American leg irons. He answered coldly. "If when the child is old enough to understand your written hand, you should pass one word of knowledge of his non-white heridity onto him, and, of course, he'll look white, he could only look white....If you tell him, I will find a place, however far, where slavery still exists as it did before the war, and I will sell your very soul away. The child will be white. There's only darkness for him if he learns that he is black. His wealth and his beauty would mean nothing. The child you bear is my child, and if you take him from me by telling him he's black, I'll take you from your own life, and I'll sell the child as well, separately,so the little nigger will never see you again."

The room was like a shattered piece of crystal, the light dimmer now and growing dark. "Oh, Jacob, forgive me. I loved you so." She could feel the baby passing out of her into the doctor's waiting hands. She never saw the baby, and given her wish to die and to take the child with her, death was hers too late for anything to matter. The slap came and her first born took breath and cried, a lovely brown skinned boy, whole and healthy and strong.

the funeral

Fans were moving all around the room; every row of hands in the funeral chapel beating out a different rhythm from the sway and swish behind or in front of it. A sister in the middle of the room began patting her foot and raised her voice in a mellow and rending sound. With her head down, her foot tapping slowly, her fan swaying in the thick hot air, she sang in slow candence, "Where He leads me, I will follow," and a brother in the next row picked up the sound and raised his voice in a hush, "Where He leads me, I will follow," the heads of the people at a slow nod, the feet almost in unison with every voice blending a black folks' death ache into the words, "Where He leads me, I will follow. And go with Him. With Him. All the way," down to a hum so soft that fan whispers breathed the hot air over the melody and the room fell to feet still beating on the sadness until the whole room was one long still place.

Carrie sat way in the back and tried not to look at the
casket. She looked down at her feet and absently
tapped her shoes together. Despite efforts to the
contrary, she thought of Willie; she had seen Willie
lying dead on her father's morgue table. Willie was
like Alfred except that there was nothing known which
could have saved Willie since he died of sickle
cell anemia. Alfred had been thrown away. A white
man had shot him in the back of his twelve year old
head three months ago. He had been tall for his age.
The white man had said he wouldn't have shot Alfred
if he'd known he was a boy rather than a man. Carrie
closed her eyes and sat back against the chair. First
John, then Alfred, now Willie; all dead in less than a
year. For the first time in her life sitting there, the
thought crossed her mind that she *really* could die;
that maybe she would not live long enough to grow up.
Carrie swallowed and wiped sweat from her brow and
nose. She had an impulse to leave the room and return
upstairs, but she knew this wouldn't work. The
housekeeper was sick and couldn't stay with her while
her parents were at the funeral. This was the only
reason she had to attend the funeral in the first place.
She closed her eyes and tried to think of something
else to push away the fear.

A man who sang in the church choir began a hymn.
"Jesus keep me near the cross," and by the time he
sang the word cross, all of the folk were singing softly
with him. "There's a pre-cious foun-tain," plaintive,
the sound, and the movement of his mouth, as with
eyes closed he eased the words into the room. Carrie
had seen Willie yesterday, a few minutes before her
father lifted him into the casket. "Free to all, a
heal-ing stream." He was dressed in a white suit with
a pale blue shirt and creme satin tie. Her daddy said
Willie had never worn clothes like that before. "Flows
from Calvary's mountain." Mr. Acre never had owned
much and it had cost him too much for Willie to be
sick. He couldn't pay the hospital. Turner said he

wasn't charging for the funeral because if Mr. Acre couldn't pay to keep Willie alive, it didn't make any sense for him to pay for the dying, when he was already with his grief. "In the Cross. In the Cross. Be my glo-ry e-ver." The boy was small; dreadfully thin, bones and sinews showing hard lines along his arms and hands and about his neck. Her father had carefully filled in the hollows at the boy's cheeks and temples with a special cream which he injected from behind the hairline with a long and very thin hypodermic needle. Willie looked healthy and strong now lying in that small white full-couch casket. Carrie's mother had combed his hair and arranged his hands across his waist after her father had made them less shriveled with cream injections. Carrie asked why they were making him look so good when he was going to be buried, and her mother said because people wanted to see him. Especially Mr. Acre; a last look at what was leaving forever. If Willie looked bad, it would make the grieving longer and deeper. That was all.

She didn't want to see Willie again. She didn't want to listen to the creaking of the lowering device which would glide Willie down into the ground. "'Til my raptured soul shall find, rest beyond the river."

A sudden hush came over the singing and everybody stood up. Carrie knew it was Mr. Acre arriving, but she couldn't see him for all of the people in front of her who were so much taller.

. . .all the moving and loading. . .the hearse door swinging shut. . .headlights and engines turned on for the procession. . . .

Carrie sat on the hearse seat between her parents, an unaccustomed solitude about her, as the huge funeral coach took them along the roads to the church where the bell began tolling, one slow tone after another. Within minutes the line was formed and the march into the church was begun.

The piano played and the choir sang, "Near the Cross, I'll watch and wait, hoping, trusting, e-ver," the choir voices in cadence to slow moving feet. The pall bearers had a light load. " 'Til I reach the gold-en strand, just beyond the ri-ver." Flower girls and the deathly sick sweetness of bruised flower petals carried in their arms, stretched ahead of the procession of bearers, the casket and the family, their feet unsure of where they would go when they reached the end of the aisle. "In the Cross. In the Cross. Be my glo-ry e-ever." Mr. Williamson, Turner's assistant, motioned the girls to either side of where the casket was to go. Carrie was on one side of Mr. Acre while her mother helped him to walk from the other. He was just a little bit of a man, all bent over.

Carrie watched her father's large hands pushing against the casket, guiding it ahead of them between walls of dark toned people turned slightly to see them go by. The smell of nervous perspiration and gingham cloth mingled in the heat and moved in heavy waves among the people. "'Til my raptured soul shall find, rest be-yond the ri-ver."

The casket came to rest below the preacher's pulpit, his voice low and calm and barely audible during the rustled whisper of seat taking. Mr. Acre and a distant cousin were the only relatives. The closed casket under a blanket of red roses and green fern seemed smaller than ever. Now that Mr. Acre was seated, Carrie started to move to a pew at the side of the church with her mother. She felt uncomfortable with him because she sensed that if she stayed she would have to be responsible for helping the old man and she didn't think that she knew how. She was frightened and it weighed much too heavily.

"Don't go, chile," he said in a hoarse whisper. Stella nodded for Carrie to stay where she was so she sat down again and closed her eyes. The room circled around and she leaned on Mr. Acre, finally opening her eyes again and looking into his face. He was crying, dry eyed. It was the look on his face: an awful look, his lips pressed tight and his nostrils not moving when he breathed. His unblinking eyes simply stared.

A deacon prayed, "Oh, Lord, deliver us from our earthly trials . . . ." The choir sang "Steal away . . . ." and the preacher pleaded with God to receive the soul of an innocent child. Reverend Brady read from the Holy Bible, 'And I gave my heart to know wisdom, and to know madness and folly; I perceived that this also is a vexation of spirit . . . . For in much wisdom is much grief, and he that increaseth knowledge increaseth sorrow.'"

Reverend Brady raised his face towards the ceiling as if seeing through the wood and shingling up past the day's storm clouds into God's place. His eyes were wide open, his lips slightly parted, his arms held out straight before him as in invocation. His black robe, worn and tired, draped down below his shoes to the floor.

"Lord. We know too well this here death; this sickness which again have struck one of your youngest childreng. We are wise in knowing that you comes to take us home to your heavenly kingdom. Folks gone we ain't never gonna see no mo'e in this life.

"But we knows another wisdom, too. And though the Holy Gospel say it's vanity too, knowledge of your greater purpose is a comfort to us."

His voice grew stronger as he began singing his preaching.

"You has come, Great Lord Almighty,
To save us from crying too hard.
You has come, Great God,
To help us know things will be better bye and
bye."

A brother spoke, "Amen," and feet began patting among the deacons and the senior choir, among the congregation sitting from front to back to the extra seats along the walls.

"We knows you has come, Sweet Jesus,
To protec' us from ourselves.
We knows, yes we knows, Sweet God,
You has come to comfort us in our hour of trial."

Sweat poured off of Reverend Brady's upturned face. He moved to his left, wiping with a handkerchief, streams of sprayed spit catching in the light from the stained glass window behind his head as he shouted,

"Lord, please take this child into your kingdom.
Please comfort his grandfather. This sweet old
man.
Make his path along the way of righteousness.
Make his days free from grief and ready for the
promised land.
Ease his mind in your words, Sweet God,
'In my House, there is many mansions, If
it were not so, I would not have told you.
He that believeth in Jesus, he also
believeth in me.'"

Reverend Brady, his face raised to heaven, shouted God to make Mr. Acre's burden light, to set it down, to give him peace. His voice simmered to a quiet, like boiling water with the heat turned slowly down to low fire. The spit ceased its flying as he spoke now and he turned ever so slowly to his left and to his right and back to center in the last whispered words, until he said, amidst the feet still beating a rhythm against the floor, "Let us pray," and ended, "Lord Jesus Almighty, receive this thy lamb into thy House and let this old man have thy comfort in his last days."

All the while, the old man held Carrie's hand. He stared at the casket and nodded his head to somebody that nobody else could see. He sat through it all and let himself be directed in his part of the viewing of the remains. Everybody who wanted took one last look

and when it was Mr. Acre's turn, he softly covered the
boy's face with the casket cowling and watched in a
daze as the lid was shut. His eyes were wet by the time
he left the church.

And then the grass of the graveside was under his feet
and the casket was going down, "Earth to earth, ashes
to ashes, and dust to dust. . . ."

He turned and moved away. He had no cane and
stumbled into people who had crowded about the
grave to see the committal service. He gently pushed
them out of his bent over way, as they motioned to
help him, and shuffled between a row of graves, trying
to get to the car. The services weren't quite over, but
he didn't seem to know, and no one could stop him.
He pulled free of Stella as she tried to take his arm. He
wouldn't listen, couldn't seem to hear. They all stood
watching, wondering in confusion what to do.

Carrie followed him involuntarily. She was drawn after
him without a conscious thought. He needed help
walking and it was a long way to the car.

Carrie reached him as he reached the car. He tried to
open the door but didn't have the strength, so he held
onto the handle and bowed his head. "Pretty day. He
was buried on such a pretty day."

"Mr. Acre...."

"Gi' 'way, child." He turned his head to the side and
looked at Carrie strangely. "You'll be a tall man when
you grows up, Willie," he said. "Look like your
Daddy. Yes, you do. Got his black skin and his mouth
and nose and his hairline and when you smiles, I
could swear you was him all over."

"Mr. Acre."

He closed his eyes and the water came down his gaunt
cheeks.

"Mr. Acre. Don't cry. Please, don't cry." And then
Carrie remembered something her mother once said

when she had fallen down and hurt herself. So
Carrie whispered to the old man, hoping that he
would hear her. "It helps to cry on somebody, Mr.
Acre. You can cry on me. It's alright."

He reached out for her and hugged her close. "You're
a good child. You gonna grow into a fine man. Hold
on and get well. You gonna grow free into a tall man
that'd make your Momma and Daddy proud."Shhh.
Hush, now. Hush. No need to cry......"

FROM PLAN TO PLANET by Haki R. Madhubuti (Don L. Lee). "This work is replete and innovative and thought provoking ideas which should lead us directly to the task before the Black race." Chancellor Williams. Cloth $4.95, Paper $2.50.

HOME IS A DIRTY STREET by Eugene Perkins. A "first" in sociological studies of Black street gangs, written by a Black man intimately involved with gang youth. This work has been called by Lerone Bennett, Jr. ". . .a profound and deeply distrubing book which should be read by every person in this troubled land. . . . His book is one of the most important on the sociology of the streets since *Black Metropolis.*" 193 pages. Paper $4.25.

GARVEY, LUMUMBA, MALCOLM: NATIONALISTS-SEPA-TISTS by Shawna Maglanbayan. A very critical reassessment of the role that Black Nationalists have played in raising the level of consciousness of Black people. Through the lives of Garvey, Lumumba and Malcolm X., Maglanbayan illuminates the strengths and weaknesses of the Black nationalist position when the dominant forces in society are mobilizing to destroy it. A serious scholarly work that leaves the reader with a clear picture of the gravity of the problems that the Black man faces in the world today. 118 pages. Cloth $4.95, Paper $2.50.

THE DESTRUCTION OF BLACK CIVILIZATION: Great Issues of a Race from 4500 B.C. to 2000 A.D. by Dr. Chancellor Williams. Now known as the "Black Bible," it is a new approach to the study of the history of the Black race that explains why we lose. Extensive bibliography, footnotes and index, 398 pages. Cloth $10.00, Paper $5.95.

THE REDEMPTION OF AFRICA AND BLACK RELIGION by St. Clair Drake. Over thirty years of teaching, publishing and research serve as background for this volume which deals with the experience of black religion in North America and the Caribbean, the role of religion in our development toward freedom and self-determination, and the development of a mode of thinking called "Ethiopianism." 80 pages. Paper $1.95.

Order from your local bookstore or directly from THIRD WORLD PRESS. Payment must accompany all orders and include $.95 handling charge.

BLACK FAIRY by Eugene (Useni) Perkins. An inspiring and enjoyable musical drama about a Black Fairy who lacks pride in herself. She is taken on an informative journey to ancient Egypt, East Afrika, a southern slave plantation and the streets of Harlem. Narration is accompanied by music throughout. In her travels the Black Fairy meets Aesop, Brer Rabbit, Brer Fox, Uncle Remus, Stag-o-lee, Leadbelly, and many other characters in Black folklore and Black history. She learns that being Black is reason to be proud. Every child should hear the Black Fairy. (record) $5.00.

JACKIE by Luevester Lewis. An adventure story of a young Black girl who moves to a new neighborhood. Excellent beginner for teaching plot construction. Simplified version of the story appears beneath each illustration. Delightfully illustrated by Cheryl Jolly. Ages 5-10, Paper $1.50.

THE TIGER WHO WORE WHITE GLOVES or WHAT YOU ARE YOU ARE by Gwendolyn Brooks. This basic reader uses rhyme and reason to focus on perenial subject of accepting what you are. It is a charming animal fable, colorful and beautifully illustrated. A must for teaching basic skills. Ages 2-8, Cloth $5.95. Paper $3.00.

COUNTRY OF THE BLACK PEOPLE by Corene Casselle. This is an exciting children's history book which will surely foster a more profound interest in Black History. Also contains meaningful geographical information. Imaginatively illustrated by Beni Casselle. Paper $3.00.

I WANT TO BE by Dexter and Patricia Oliver. A multi-purpose alphabet reader depicting Black children engaged in occupations ranging from Architect to Zoologist. The book also emphasizes vocabulary and makes the child aware of vocations to which they can aspire. Can be read to the younger child as well as read by children ages 8-12. Illustrations also make handsome bulletin board displays. Cloth $5.95, Paper $2.95.

I LOOK AT ME by Mari Evans. Excellent beginning reader for pre-schoolers. Abundant positive visual images. A vocabulary list and instructions on many other ways to derive the maximum from this helpful book are included. Cloth $4.95, Paper $1.95.

Mail to: *THIRD WORLD PRESS*
             7524   Cottage Grove
             Chicago IL 60619